THE AUTHOR HAS RATED THIS NARRATIVE

RL-13

INAPPROPRIATE FOR CHILDREN UNDER 13

For the real-time portrayal of a brutal murder by firearm, the descriptive mutilation and dismemberment of a human body, discussion of illegal narcotics, and some profanity.

Also by R.L. Akers

OVERTWIXT

Overtwixt*: Welcome to the World of Bridges* ‡

Escape from Overtwixt ‡

Overtwixt 3: The Kaiserlands*

The Circus of Dagmør *(Golden Age, book 1)*

The Heroes of Centhule *(Golden Age, book 2)*

The King of Caymerlot *(Golden Age, book 3)*

Scavenger Hunt • *Perilous Flight*
The Princess & Her Throne (chapter book) ‡
The Knight & His Friends (picture book)

LEGACY of ATLANTIS

Atlantis*: Twilight of Mankind*

The GRYPHENS SAGA

Prometheus Rebound

Prometheus Revealed

Prometheus Rising
(short story collection)

FROM THE FILES OF

Gray Gaynes #7

A NEW HORIZON...

GRAY DAWN

THE CASE OF THE FOOLPROOF FRATRICIDE

A NOVELLA BY

RL AKERS

ISBN-13: 979-8-9933732-2-5

Also by R.L. Akers

From the Files of
GRAY GAYNES

Gray in the City: †‡

Gray Tones ‡

Gray Area ‡

Old Gray ‡

Gray Matter

Gray Rose

Fade to Gray

Gray in the Dark:

Gray Dawn

*Gray Stakes**

---

*forthcoming
† anthology edition
‡ available on audiobook

For John Paul,

who always showed such interest
in whatever project I was working on

Gray Gaynes

"Grayson Gaynes" redirects here.

Gray Gaynes (born Grayson Thom Gaynes; June 14, 1987) is an American retired New York City Police Department (NYPD) detective, best known for his controversial involvement in the hunt for the Mad Batter serial killer.[1][2] On March 1, 2016, during the course of the Mad Batter investigation, Gaynes was recorded beating a handcuffed suspect on livestream video.[3][4][5] The footage went viral, with millions of views by the end of that week.[?]

Despite his dubious public image, Gaynes has been described as highly intelligent and analytical, an "outside the box" thinker with a commitment to finding the truth, no matter how long it takes. Among his coworkers in the NYPD Detective Bureau, he had a reputation for liking "strange" cases—homicides with an apparent element of the paranormal, even if the truth always proved more mundane.[6]

Early Life

Little is publicly known of Gaynes' childhood. He was born and raised in New York City, most likely spending the majority of his time in the Manhattan borough.[7] Even less is known of his mother, who was deceased by 2007.[?] Gaynes' father, "Old" Gray Gaynes, was later convicted of various white collar crimes and sentenced to 10 years in prison, of which he served 7.[8][9]

Gaynes graduated high school in 2004 (having skipped a grade) and undergraduate university in December 2007.[10] He earned a Bachelor of Arts degree in English Literature.[?]

Gaynes married Rose Moynihan on April 5, 2014.[11]

In 2015, Gaynes was attacked in Central Park and later hospitalized as a result of injuries sustained. His wife did not survive the attack.[12]

Career

On July 2, 2008, Gaynes joined the NYPD as a probationary patrolman. During this supervised period of his career, he cooperated with federal authorities in a "sting" against his father, playing an instrumental role in the elder Gray Gaynes' arrest.[13] This proved to be a career-making move, resulting in a "glowing recommendation" from FBI special agent Jackson Pinder that paved the way for Gaynes' rapid advancement within the NYPD.[?] Performance reviews from that time described Gaynes as "keen[-minded] and analytical... capable of decisive action, and cool under pressure."[14]

Gaynes joined the homicide squad of the NYPD

Detective Bureau in June 2013 upon his promotion to detective third grade[15] (the initial, lowest detective rank). He partnered with several other detectives on different cases, but usually Patrick “Mack” McMurphy.[16] He quickly developed a reputation for methodical investigation ("overly-methodical," according to some fellow detectives).[6] In January 2015, Gaynes was assigned for the first time to the Mad Batter investigation,[2] the biggest case of his career,[?] when he received an anonymous tip regarding the location of Ann-Marie Toscani’s body (one of the Mad Batter’s victims). The tipster had asked for Gaynes by name. That investigation stalled months later, in April, when Gaynes’ chief suspect "alibied out."[1][2] Soon thereafter, Gaynes himself went on medical leave following the Central Park attack, which detectives at the time ruled unrelated, a "mugging gone wrong."[12]

After returning from leave, Gaynes worked a number of cases of an unusual nature, developing a further reputation for "liking the strange ones."[6] He was assigned once more to the Mad Batter case after the February 24, 2016 murder of Alyssa Lori, who the press immediately reported as a possible Mad Batter victim.[17] The re-opened Mad Batter investigation proved to be Gaynes’ final case as an NYPD detective.[2] Despite some community backlash (due to the widely-publicized beating, as well as other erratic behavior), Gaynes was allowed to retire from the NYPD and receives full pension benefits.[4]

Last edited on 30 October 2021 at 13:13

Notable Cases

- The Mad Batter (January–April 2015, February–March 2016)
- The Barton Chan elevator slaying (May 2015)
- The so-called Hellhound Homicide (August–December 2015)
- Oswald Parker's "spontaneous combustion" (December 2015–January 2016)
- The wrongful death of Alan Null, founding partner of Taurus Torus (February 2016)

Medical Conditions

During the Mad Batter trial and resulting media circus, it was revealed that Gaynes suffers from several neurological conditions arising from injuries sustained during the 2015 Central Park attack:[2][18]

- Achromatopsia (colloquially known as color blindness)
- Hemeralopia (day blindness, the inability to see clearly in bright light)
- Prosopagnosia (face blindness, the inability to recognize what should be familiar faces)

Any one of these conditions makes an individual unfit for service as a police officer,[19] which is why Gaynes later admitted to hiding these disabilities from his superiors for almost a year following the attack.[?] When the truth came out, Gaynes was forced into early retirement; but despite his subterfuge, he was allowed to receive pension benefits precisely because his injuries were received in the execution of his duties as a police officer.[4] (The Central Park attack came as a direct result of Gaynes' Mad Batter investigation.)

Life after the NYPD

Since retiring, Gaynes has fallen out of the public eye. Multiple sources have suggested he left New York City entirely,[19][20] and former love interest Vera Vecoli claims Gaynes and his father have been "roadtripping their way west," picking up itinerant work along the way.[21] Appearing briefly on a webisode of the short-lived series *Whatever Happened to that Guy?*, Vecoli said:

> I'm pleased to report that father and son continue working to repair their relationship, but there's a lot of hurt there, a lotta baggage. But please, the best thing you can do for them is give them their space. Gray[son] Gaynes has done a lot for this city, and he's no longer a public servant. He's a private citizen now, and he deserves his privacy, y'know?[21]

GRAY DAWN

Pronunciation Guide

Iñupiaq – in-YOO-pee-awk
(*pl.* Iñupiat – in-YOO-pee-awt)
— an Alaskan Inuit

Utqiaġvik – oot-kee-AWG-vik
— largest Iñupiaq village and borough seat,
known as Barrow until 2016,
northernmost settlement in the United States

Nuiqsut – NOO-eek-suht
— smaller Iñupiaq village,
150 miles southeast of Utqiaġvik

tunnuq – TUHN-uhk
— Iñupiaq word for a non-Iñupiaq

Thursday, December 7th
U-Turn, Alaska

The aurora borealis glinted colorlessly off the windshields of the parked work trucks, the Northern Lights somehow magnificent even when reduced to gray tones.

Grayson Gaynes, TrephOil roughneck 'fifth hand,' hiked up one leg of his heavy coverall pants and kicked his boot heel against a truck tire—dislodging the stubborn clod of permafrost muck that impeded his gait. Straightening once more, he glanced both ways before crossing the street.

He wasn't checking for traffic. He was checking for bears, which were known to roam freely through this semi-permanent oil field work camp known as U-Turn. It was a hell of a thing, seeing a grizzly or polar bear covered with trash as it rummaged through a dumpster. But there were no bears in sight this time, so Gray continued on his way, trudging across the frozen-dirt road. He wasn't the only *human* out and about, but no one loitered long in these temperatures, even at the most active times of the day.

Aside from the light show above—and the occasional bear—there was little exciting about U-Turn, Alaska. A couple dozen modular buildings: offices, dorms, and cafeterias suspended above gravel pads. A fleet of diesel crew-cab work trucks plugged in and heated even when not in use, lest their batteries die or their oil freeze to gel. And, of course, this single dirt track road running through camp. No, not *through* camp; there was a reason they called this place U-Turn. When the rare commercial freight hauler arrived overland from the outside world, it had no option but to turn around to get back out again—retracing TrephOil's spur road to the long, winter-only access trail that connected Utqiaġvik with Prudhoe Bay.

In short, this place was the opposite of New York City, where Gray once lived and worked as a homicide detective. For that reason alone, he loved it. That and the fact that his day blindness was a non-issue during the months-long darkness of winter above the Arctic Circle. U-Turn had seen its last sunset of the year two weeks prior; and though there were still a few hours of murky twilight around noon each day, the sun itself wouldn't reappear until late January (and even then, for less than an hour).

The only building in U-Turn that wasn't dirty or pre-fabricated—in other words, the only cheerful destination for fifty miles—was Dawn's place. A simple clapboard structure on stilts, it was painted bright yellow (or so he'd been told) with a big fiery sunrise depicted in red on one windowless wall. And though it was the closest thing U-Turn had to a restaurant, it didn't officially have a name. It was simply the place where a woman named Dawn offered modestly priced home-cooked meals and a taste of normality between shifts—something many of the oil field workers longed for.

Including Gray himself. Grateful at the prospect of warmth, for body *and* soul, he shuffled up the ramp and eagerly rubbed his boots on the block at the door, scraping off more of the ubiquitous mud and dust. That done, he pulled fabric booties over his shoes and stepped inside, closing the door quickly behind him. Removing the filthy boots entirely was not an option, not if he wanted to keep his toes.

"Gray!" called an upbeat voice. "Come in, take a load off. Your favorite table is open."

Unzipping his parka and pulling the fleece trapper hat from his head, Gray surveyed the crowd and quickly picked out the speaker. Despite his face blindness—his inability to identify friends or acquaintances on sight, something most people managed intuitively—Gray actually *did* recognize *this* woman. Not her face so much as the tattoos inked upon it: a V-shape pattern emerging from her hairline to point at her nose; arcs crossing both cheeks; and five thin vertical stripes drawn from lower lip over her chin.

Dawn Atiqtalik Simmonds was Iñupiaq, a member of the Alaskan Inuit people. And if her unique facial markings weren't a dead giveaway of her identity, her broad smile might be all by itself.

Gray smiled genuinely in return. "Dawn, good morning. Colder than usual today, I think."

She gave a generous chuckle, though she heard weak jests about the cold and dark almost constantly from tunnuq—non-Iñupiat men like Gray. "Ready for some dinner?"

"Please!" Gray said enthusiastically.

She waved him to his preferred corner booth, where he pulled a well-worn paperback from one pocket before tossing parka and hat onto the opposite seat. Then he settled into his own high-backed bench and groaned, taking that load off as Dawn suggested.

It had been a long shift—they all were—working through the night from 6 p.m. to 6 a.m. It was Gray's third season on the oil fields of the National Petroleum Reserve in Alaska, or NPR-A. He'd started as a roustabout, doing unskilled labor and whatever odd jobs were needed, only this winter being promoted to roughneck or 'fifth hand.' Maybe he could have earned that promotion faster, but the fact was he liked the variety of work and relative lack of responsibility that came with an unskilled position. And when added to his NYPD pension, the pay was more than adequate.

But the work *was* hard, physically taxing even if not for the extreme conditions. A hot meal at Dawn's was his daily reward, and tonight that meal was a hearty plate of meat and potatoes, the reindeer flank steak slathered in a savory sauce. He read from *David Copperfield* as he ate, trying not to spatter the ratty pages with too much gravy.

Dickens' semi-autobiography had become one of Gray's favorites, for he identified with its hero in so many ways, not least the tragic death of his wife so early in their marriage. Gray could only hope he emerged from his own challenges with half the positive attitude of Copperfield. He was certainly trying.

This existence on Alaska's North Slope was hard, but it was also a simple, honest life. More than seven years had passed since Gray Gaynes last investigated a homicide, and longer since his own wife was brutally murdered. He would trade that emotional toll for physical toil any day. Transplanting here, he had finally experienced some healing.

All too soon, his meal was done, and he waved off Dawn's offer of a second plate. He was already suitably drowsy. Carefully marking the place in his book, he sat back, content to people-watch.

The place was about three-fourths full 'tonight,' maybe twenty-five customers—all oil field workers like Gray, of course. A fair number sat at other mismatched tables that ringed the perimeter, but only because every barstool was occupied. That bar was Dawn's true pride and joy, an actual, lacquered, live-edge wooden surface that ran the length of the building. Not that Dawn served any booze here. In deference to local dry laws—and for practical reasons—alcohol was prohibited in U-Turn. The workers who frequented this place before or after their shifts were here for the food, whatever rich meals Dawn chose to prepare (one breakfast option and one dinner option each day; there was no menu). The fact that Dawn offered a variety of glass-bottled soda pops and non-alcoholic beers, even a few mocktails, was simply a bonus.

Dawn's place *was*, to be frank, a dive. Poorly lit and with no windows, its dinginess was enlivened year-round by strands of Christmas lights—the old school chunky bulb variety, not LEDs. A jukebox played 80s and 90s rock lightly in one corner. And somehow, between those simple touches and that beautiful wooden bar, the place became homey and warm. Certainly, the atmosphere beat the hell out of the sterile, fluorescent-lit cafeterias the company employees ate at most of the time. And almost all of Dawn's regulars loved her for it.

Gray picked out the problem customer almost immediately. Booze or no, he was acting the part of the drunk, obviously accustomed to using that lack of inhibition as an excuse to behave poorly. With Gray's condition, there was no way to know if he'd actually met the guy before, but he rather doubted it. Probably a roustabout, one of this season's new hires. The man was talking loudly, shoulder-bumping his barstool neighbors in an overly friendly—and unrequited—manner, and banging his glass for a refill.

Ignoring his antics, Dawn made her rounds of the tables with a tea pitcher in each hand, sweet and unsweet. Topping off Gray's glass (unsweet, of course), she asked, "How's your dad? Still down in Anchorage?"

Gray shook his head in wonder. There were three hundred workers operating out of U-Turn at any given time, alternating in two-week 'hitches' with another group of three hundred on break down south. Sure, not all of them came through Dawn's place, but the woman clearly had a gift if she could remember a personal tidbit Gray had shared just once, last season. "Old Gray's doing well, thank you," he confirmed with a smile. "We share a house in Eagle River"—a suburb of Anchorage—"where he does a lot of reading, sipping his tea, going out to eat. Retirement... suits him," Gray concluded diplomatically.

"Like father, like son," Dawn smiled, indicating Gray's own book and tea glass.

"Ha," Gray snorted. "No, always hot tea in his case."

"Earl *Grey*, I assume?" There was a sparkle in her eye.

Gray laughed delightedly. "Probably. He can be a bit pretentious. Dresses to impress, even if he never plans to leave the house."

Behind Dawn, the problem customer had begun banging his glass more insistently. With a mischievous smile, the young Iñupiaq woman pointedly ignored the fellow. “Sounds like Old Gray is a character.”

“You have no idea. What about you? Do you have family?”

“No,” Dawn said promptly, then hesitated. “Well, not really. Parents are passed, and...” She looked a little guilty and shrugged, not elaborating further. With a sigh, she finally turned back to the bar. “Anyway, let me know if you need anything.”

The impatient bombast, whose stool was near the end of the bar closest to Gray, was now out of his seat. He seized Dawn’s arm as she tried to pass, causing her to slosh a fair volume of tea onto the floor. “What’s a man gotta do to get some service around here?” he very nearly slurred.

Dawn smirked. “I don’t know. Being more polite might be a good start.” This drew snickers from some of the other men. Gray himself watched the confrontation carefully, though he knew Dawn didn’t need rescue.

The man was unamused. “I want another beer. Now.”

“I think you’ve had one too many O’Doul’s already,” Dawn told him drily. “I’m cutting you off.”

The idiot’s expression turned ugly, but then he hesitated, noticing something for the first time. “That’s an awfully big gun for a little lady,” he actually said.

Ah yes, the revolver holstered securely at Dawn's hip. Alaska was an open carry state, no permit or registration required. Gray himself didn't carry anymore, not since that business in the Catskills seven-plus years ago, and oil field workers weren't allowed to do so anyway. But almost all of the locals seemed to.

In Dawn's case, that weapon appeared to be a Ruger Super Redhawk, a popular choice on the North Slope. Probably chambered with .44 Magnum 240 grain, specifically designed to stop a bear. An awfully big gun indeed.

"You compensating for something?" the idiot roustabout wanted to know.

Tea pitcher still gripped in each hand, one arm immobilized by the lout, Dawn actually threw back her head and laughed genuinely. "Of course I'm compensating. Aside from the bears, I'm one of... what, twenty women in this camp? I won't win an arm wrestling match against any of you men, so yeah; I kinda like the idea of carrying a weapon that can take a fellow's head clean off if needed." She inclined her chin and smiled sweetly. "But that's not needed *today*, is it?"

The man looked like he might disagree, but then he felt a hand on one shoulder—someone intervening. Dawn wouldn't like that. She really didn't need rescuing, and it might encourage future troublemakers if they thought she did. Regardless, the roustabout turned with a sneer... and froze. “Oh, um, Mr. Thrasher.”

Gray straightened. Thrasher? That was the company man, the top-ranking official for Treadgold-Phelps Oil in the North Slope, and what passed for mayor of U-Turn. Of course Gray couldn’t recognize him, but everyone else would.

“Release Ms. Simmonds and apologize,” Thrasher said quietly.

The bully quickly did so. “Uh, sorry, Dawn. I was just thirsty, you know?”

“I completely understand,” she replied with half a smile. “Just use your manners next time, okay?”

“Yeah, I guess.”

“Another O’Doul’s for you then?”

The fellow blinked in surprise. “Uh, yeah, that’d be great.”

“Coming right up. As soon as you clean up this mess you made.” Now Dawn was smiling fully. “Let me get you a mop.” And only then did she casually retreat behind the bar, like nothing significant had happened. And truth to tell, nothing really had. These kinds of encounters weren’t that unusual considering the rough-edged, predominantly male population of a work camp like this. Refusing to be intimidated, Dawn had a way of turning bullies into allies with her smile and wit.

She returned with a mop and bucket moments later, to find Thrasher still waiting... along with another man Gray hadn't noticed until right then.

This other man wore a police uniform.

Dawn eyed the cop, the sole representative of the NSBPD—the North Slope Borough Police Department—here in U-Turn. "Abe," she greeted him warily.

"Dawn," he responded simply, his expression unreadable.

"Sorry about this," Thrasher interjected, gesturing to the roustabout who was now mopping the floor with unpracticed motions. "I'll make a notation in his file—"

Dawn waved a dismissive hand. "Please don't. It's really nothing." She jerked her head back toward the cop. "What's going on? Abe here has the look of a man ready to be ill."

Abraham Kanayurak had no tattoos, though Gray knew he was Iñupiaq too. And he did indeed have a sick look about him, which Gray recognized all too well from his own years with the NYPD.

Hesitating, solicitous, Abe produced a manila envelope and pulled out a glossy 8x10 photo. "Does this look familiar?" he asked Dawn simply.

She glanced at the photo briefly, then scowled. "Sure. That's David's wristwatch."

The cop traded a look with Thrasher.

"What?" Dawn demanded. "Did someone finally rob it from him or something?" Her usually friendly face was uncharacteristically sour.

"No," Abe allowed, "at least, we don't think so. The watch was found. We wanted to make sure it was David's."

"Yeah, definitely," Dawn confirmed without bothering to look at the photo again.

"And when was the last time you spoke with your brother?"

Dawn's eyes slid toward Gray, looking guilty. She was thinking how she'd dodged his question earlier, about family. Obviously Dawn's relationship with her brother was complicated.

Gray was more interested in Abe Kanayurak's behavior. The police officer was obviously here investigating, and not as part of any mere stolen property case. The man was tense. He had bad news to deliver, and little experience doing so. But why was he doing this *now*, so late at night?

Because he wasn't, Gray immediately reminded himself. Objectively speaking, it was morning right now—about 8:15 a.m., judging from the neon-trimmed analog clock on Dawn's wall. It only felt like evening because Gray was coming off night shift, which was easy to forget since the sun never made an appearance anyway. Dawn's own work shift was even more complicated, serving breakfast from 4 to 6 a.m. *and* 4 to 6 p.m. (before each of the 12-hour shifts) and pivoting to dinner from 6 to 9 a.m. and 6 to 9 p.m. (to accommodate workers coming *off* those shifts). But for anyone on a normal schedule—like Thrasher and Abe—the workday was only just beginning.

"The last time I talked with David?" Dawn repeated, pausing to think. "Months ago. September, before he motored south for the winter."

Abe nodded, scribbling a note in a small spiralbound notebook. "Aboard the *Bowhead*?"

Somehow her scowl deepened. "Exactly. Have you ever met David? You at least know who he is, right? That marine biologist everyone always complains about—driving that flashy big boat around, the kind that doesn't belong up here?"

"Uh huh," Abe said noncommittally. "And September was the last time you spoke with him?"

"Yeah." Dawn glanced back and forth between Abe and Thrasher. "Why? What's this all about? And what's it got to do with David's wristwatch?"

"Well, we—that is to say, the NSBPD—don't think your brother ever did motor south." Abe opened his mouth to say more, and for a moment, nothing came out.

Here it was. Dawn sensed it too, and her face began clouding.

"See, that watch..." Abe said, taking a different tack. "Someone shot a problem bear outside Nuiqsut earlier this week. It was hassling the locals, you see, attacked a child." He was rambling, not wanting to get to the point. “Anyway, we did a necropsy—like an autopsy, but on an animal, you know?—and, um...” He spit out the rest in a rush. “And we found your brother’s watch in its gullet, along with human remains.”

Dawn reeled—actually, physically staggering until Thrasher caught and steadied her.

“I’m sorry to have to tell you this, Dawn,” Abe said genuinely. “But we think your brother is dead.”

Gray did not rest well that night. Tossing and turning, he kept reliving the most difficult next-of-kin notifications he himself had delivered during his career as a homicide detective. Worse yet, his subconscious invoked the nightmare of waking in that hospital room eight years ago, when he learned about his own wife's murder for the first time.

Finally giving up around 3:30 p.m.—yes, that same calendar day, but really a new day from his perspective—Gray sat up and turned the light on. His depressingly tiny but blessedly private dorm room swam into view, little more than a twin size bed, desk/chair combo, and narrow closet. Rubbing his eyes, he grabbed some clothes and a towel, then stepped into the hall. Unfortunately, the bathrooms were *not* private, but at this hour he wouldn't need to fight over hot water, at least. Gray didn't bother locking his room; no one here did.

By 4, he was feeling slightly more human. Since he had more time than usual this 'morning,' he bypassed his usual coffee and breakfast at the company-owned dining hall (only stopping briefly to pack his lunch), intending to check on Dawn instead.

He didn't typically start his day at Dawn's place, and honestly, he had little in the way of a personal relationship with the woman. But after last night... well, he felt a deep sense of empathy for her. Having been told of her brother's untimely death, she had pushed her way out of the establishment, leaving it to her part-time helper Ephron to close up shop. Neither Abe Kanayurak nor any of the TrephOil employees had chased after her, and Gray certainly hadn't. Sometime in the night, however, he had resolved to speak with her. Gray had some rare perspective on what she was going through, and Dawn should know he was available as a listening ear.

But when Gray arrived at Dawn's, he found the door locked, a simple handwritten note stapled to the building's wood paneling:

Gone to Nuiqsut

Back in a few days

Gray couldn't help but smile at the sign. As a general (unspoken) rule, Dawn's place was open every day of the week from November through April—the winter drilling season—but she *did* sometimes take days off. When that happened, typically with no advance warning, she simply posted one of these signs the day of. Though Dawn had some part-time help running her little establishment, it wasn't enough to keep the doors open when she herself was gone.

As for traveling to Nuiqsut, that made sense. It was the closest permanent settlement, roughly fifty or sixty miles east as the snowmobile trekked. Not only was it where that problem bear was shot—and David Simmonds' watch found—it was also, if Gray recalled, where Dawn grew up. (Her brother too, presumably.) And if David was unmarried, that made Dawn his closest surviving relative. It would fall to her to identify the man's remains, assuming there was enough to identify, and collect his watch and other belongings. Gray wasn't familiar with Iñupiat funerary customs, but he imagined responsibility for planning the disposition of those remains would fall to her too.

Saddened on behalf of the young Iñupiaq proprietor, Gray went about his day.

He met his crew on the shuttle bus at the usual place, navigating the mass of workers boarding multiple vehicles headed for different drilling sites. Settling into his usual seat, he smiled at the punchline to one of the usual jokes. They were only a couple days into their two-week hitch at this point, so spirits were still high. Gray knew from experience that guys would start getting snippy or incommunicative as the exhaustion of 12-hour workdays compounded, so humor was important—and Motormouth Miller was only too happy to meet this basic human need.

"So a man walks into a bar in New York City," Miller said loudly, starting yet another witty yarn as everyone awaited the bus's departure. "Don't ask me the guy's name or what he was drinking, but—oh, hey, Gaynes. I didn't see you there."

"Miller," Gray acknowledged, not buying it.

"Say, *you're* from New York City, yeah?"

"You know that I am." It was pretty much *all* the crew knew of his past, certainly not that he was a widower and retired cop.

"So tell me, what's the guy's name?" Miller asked. "This man who walks into a bar in New York City?"

Gray chuckled. "Let's go with... Mack."

"And what's Mack drinking?"

"A pint of Sam Adams, definitely."

Miller's nose scrunched a little at this, but he rolled with it, turning back to the bus at large. "So a guy named Mack walks into a bar in New York City, and he orders three pints of Sam Adams. *Three* pints, mind you, all at once. Drinks all three, one after another. This goes on for a few weeks, whenever Mack goes to that bar, always three pints.

"Finally, the bartender asks him: 'Why always three pints, all at once?' And Mack says, 'Oh, I have these two buddies. My pal Gaynes is working the oil fields in Alaska, and my other buddy—'" Miller stopped, glancing at Gray.

"Uh... Bobbi," Gray provided.

"'And my other buddy Bobby up and joined the navy.'"

"Not likely," Gray laughed. "Not really her thing."

"Shut up, Gaynes. So where was I? Oh right, Mack says, 'My buddy Gaynes is on the slope and my buddy Bobby's on a boat, and neither one of them's allowed to partake of fermented beverages.'" The assembled oil field workers laughed a little. No one loved being told they couldn't drink in their downtime here, but it was what it was. "'So,' Mack tells this bartender, 'I promised I would do their drinking for them, for as long as they were gone.' This makes perfect sense to the bartender, so he stops asking questions.

"Then one day, Mack comes in and orders only *two* pints. And from then on, it was only two. Concerned, the bartender eventually asks him, 'Is everything okay with your buddies? Something didn't happen to Gaynes, did it? I've heard life on an oil field is dangerous.'"

The men in the shuttle bus guffawed at this, though this whole story was a familiar setup.

"'Nah, Gaynes is just fine,' Mack replies. 'A bit weird, wastes his time reading books by dudes hundreds of years dead, but in good enough health. And Bobby is okay too, so far as I know.'" Miller winked, and Gray gave the ghost of a smile. "'Then why only two beers?' the bartender asks." Miller fell silent, glancing around at the expectant faces of the other oil field workers. "Well?" he demanded finally. "What did Mack say to the bartender?"

"'I told my wife I'd stop drinking!'" the workers chimed in, delivering the well-known punchline in near-unison. Then everyone laughed, especially a few of the newer roustabouts, who'd obviously never heard that one before. It was really for their benefit that Miller retold it, after all.

"Hey Rourke, where are *you* from?" Miller asked one of the new guys.

"Quincy, Florida!"

"Oh. I was gonna say, next time, that's where the man walks into a bar, but... do they even have bars in Quincy?"

"About as many as U-Turn!"

More laughter. Motormouth Miller kept up a steady stream of bawdy jokes and edgy stories as the bus finally got underway, easing down the dirt road and out of camp. Some of it was reused material ("What did the hole in the ground say to the oil rig?—I'm bored!"), and that was fine. A lot of roustabouts only lasted one season on the slope, so every winter saw fresh faces. But plenty of Miller's routine was original too. Gray honestly didn't know where the man got new material, day-in and day-out. He probably spent an hour scouring the Internet every night before shuteye.

Soon U-Turn was in the bus's rearview mirror, and they began the slow, 10-mile journey to their rig—which would require half an hour at the speed they were forced to drive on the packed-down snow road. Gray's eyes traced the miles of above-ground transmission pipelines for a while, then stared off across the almost-flat tundra, which faded quickly in the gloomy distance. It was crazy to think that during the summer, much of this terrain was actually crisscrossed by narrow waterways, making shallow-drafted boats the best way to get around. Then every winter, when the water froze over entirely—as far out as fifty miles from shore!—massive snowcats spent weeks recreating these snow roads from scratch.

They passed a few of TrephOil's other drilling sites on the way, some retired, others in full operation: clusters of industrial structures and still more modulars, clumped around derricks, all of it bathed by bright spotlights. The active sites were made obvious by the presence of gated checkpoints manned by company security personnel. Locals and even tourists or journalists (rare though they were) were not permitted to enter, for safety reasons.

When the bus finally passed through security at their own site, Toolpusher Tim got the crew started on today's assignments. Yes, that was actually his name, and that was actually what an oil rig's senior on-site supervisor was called. There was also the driller and his assistant running around giving orders, and the derrickman who climbed up in the superstructure to manage the mud-driller. The mud logger, the machinist, the wireman, even an EMT just in case—a guy named Cedrick that Gray rather liked. Company man Thrasher made an appearance most shifts, though he oversaw *all* of TrephOil's wellsites on this field, so he seldom stayed long. And of course there was Motormouth Miller, so-named in part because he *was* the crew's 'motorman'—the specialist in charge of maintaining all the rig's pumps and engines. The rig itself was sardonically known as Ole Orful.

As for Gray, he was down near the bottom of the pecking order. He and the other roughnecks worked on the rig's drill floor, one of the most dangerous places to be, with equipment and pipes and chains constantly swinging around. Constant vigilance was critical to maintaining safety, though Miller still found opportunities to play a prank now and then. His antics were never truly dangerous, and in their own way, they actually kept the men alert. Last and least among all the workers were the roustabouts, the unskilled laborers who did whatever cleaning or run-and-fetch tasks anyone asked of them.

The cold was the biggest danger. That night shift, it got down to the negative twenties—and with steady 10 mph flurries from the northeast, windchill was below -40° Fahrenheit. As gentle breezes went, it was brutal... and the workers were subjected to all of it, only partially sheltered from the elements by surrounding buildings. Their best protection was multiple layers of clothing, every inch of flesh kept covered, faces too. Gray even wore multiple pairs of gloves, though he had to keep changing the innermost pair whenever his own sweat started freezing to his hands. He tried to forget that temps were only going to drop further as the season progressed.

Fortunately, the constant strenuous labor also helped keep his body warm—or at least less dangerously cold. And whenever there was a momentary lull in work, he and others would drop and do pushups. Actual breaks were brief and taken inside, because his body's fluids needed to be replenished, and a cup of water would freeze instantly outside. Whenever they did retreat indoors, the men scarfed down granola bars and other snacks to keep their energy up. Lunch was whatever calorie-rich fare they had packed at the cafeteria that morning; in Gray's case, a thick roast beef wrap, two bananas, and a bag of large nuts—foods he could handle with numb fingers. He washed it all down with a thermos of strong tea. By this point in the shift, just past midnight, he needed the caffeine.

After lunch—a mere half hour break—Toolpusher Tim barked an order, and everyone filed back out. Miller cracked another joke on the way, and the crew laughed... but the sound was muffled by all those layers of gaiters and balaclavas they wore beneath their impact-resistant face shields.

By 6 a.m. quitting time, Gray's body was complaining it had reached its limit. And yet he knew he'd be wise to spend some time at the company gym facilities before bed, working muscle groups that *hadn't* been used today. He didn't want to think about that right now, though. First he was jonesing for a hot meal and some down time.

Back at U-Turn almost an hour later, Gray climbed off the bus and began his daily trudge toward Dawn's place. A couple other men turned the same direction, though most headed for one of the company-owned dining halls (unlike at Dawn's, meals there were actually free to employees), and a few guys raced to the dorm to fight over the shower. Unwinding at Dawn's was the only option for Gray, though, an almost nightly ritual since arriving in the North Slope two years ago. That habit was so thoroughly ingrained, and he was so mentally exhausted, that he completely forgot Dawn's place was closed until he got there and saw the handwritten sign again.

One of the two men with him cursed. It wasn't fifty yards back to their dorm from here, but it still felt like a monumental waste of effort given the day they'd had. The third man, scowling openly, dug a sharpie from a pocket of his coveralls and made an addition to Dawn's sign:

Gone to Nuiqsut

Back in a few days

With a sigh, Gray turned and followed the others to the overly-sterile, fluorescent-lit company cafeteria. It was going to be a *long* few days.

Monday, December 11th

U-Turn

Dawn's place was still closed Saturday afternoon before shift, and Gray didn't get another chance to drop by over the weekend. But Monday morning after work, he heard the welcome news as he and his dorm hallmates were jockeying for shower time: Dawn was back. Gray set an alarm for early wakeup and was waiting at her door by 3:45 that afternoon, a quarter hour before her normal p.m. opening time.

Hunkering down within his parka, Gray berated himself for showing up so early. This was the warmest time of day and it still felt like -20° F when you accounted for windchill. That was practically balmy compared to the negative forties he had suffered in recent night shifts, but... well, twenty-below was still twenty-below, not the sort of weather he normally chose to endure if avoidable. Rubbing his hands together through his gloves, he inspected the four-foot-tall stylized sunrise Dawn had painted in red on her yellow building. It was all just shades of gray to him, but even color blind, he could still appreciate the loving care she'd put into each lick of flame that curled out from that celestial fireball. Gray usually just blew right past the mural—everybody did—in a hurry to get inside and thaw out. The fact that Dawn would take the time to paint such elaborate flourishes anyway said something about her.

Idly, he found himself pondering the mystery that was Dawn Simmonds. She was such an atypical member of the oil field community, and not only because she was female and Native Alaskan, in a predominantly male tunnuq populace. The woman's personality, her *smile* shone all the more brightly amidst the rough and tumble crowd of laborers. Even her name was ironic for a person born this far north of the Arctic Circle, considering whole months passed in winter here without a single sunrise.

Gray waited the better part of twenty minutes, shivering and stomping. But like her namesake, Dawn never made an appearance.

Instead, it was Abraham Kanayurak who appeared just before 4 p.m. At least, Gray *assumed* it was Abe, for the man was dressed in the uniform of the North Slope Borough Police Department, and there was only one NSBPD officer in U-Turn most of the time.

Abe gave Gray a solemn nod and proceeded to staple an updated sign over top of Dawn's handwritten note. This one had been computer-printed in Times New Roman, all bold and all caps, the sheet of printer paper laminated:

cLOSED iNDEFINATELY

Questions? Call 907-555-0161

Gray pulled out his smartphone—for which he, like many 'slopers,' had satellite service—and did a quick Internet search. Apparently, this was a non-emergency number connected to NSBPD headquarters in Utqiaġvik.

Which begged the question of *why*.

U-Turn's sole cop was already trudging away. "Wait, Abe," Gray called. "What's this all about?"

Abe turned, cocked his head at Gray, then glanced pointedly at the sign.

Gray gave him a patient smile. "I'm not asking them. I'm asking you." His smile faded. "What's up with Dawn? Is she okay?"

"I can't talk about it," the cop said.

Gray felt his old instincts tingling. "Police business?"

Abe gave a slow nod, clearly out of his depth and unsure how he was expected to behave in this situation.

"You can tell me," Gray found himself saying. "I used to be a cop myself."

Abe looked at him skeptically. "You?"

"Yeah, NYPD."

Skepticism deepened to amused disbelief.

Gray sighed. Wondering why he was even doing this—he'd gone to such lengths to find a fresh, anonymous start in this place—he said, "Look me up." He gestured with his smartphone, pantomiming another Internet search. "Grayson Gaynes, retired NYPD detective." Gray actually had an official ID issued by the State of New York that proved exactly this, as well as a badge stamped RETIRED, but he was hardly in the habit of carrying either one around. Fortunately (or maybe unfortunately), there was another way to convince the man. "Seriously," he repeated, "look me up."

So Abe did. And of course, search results quickly directed the local cop to Gray's short but informative wiki article. The former NYPD detective watched the NSBPD officer's eyebrows climb as he skimmed. "*Homicide* detective!" Abe exclaimed at one point, then, "The Mad Batter case!? Wait, that was *you* on that old video—"

"Yes," Gray admitted. "Not my finest moment." Inwardly, he was groaning. The video Abe referred to, of Gray beating a handcuffed suspect, was undoubtedly still online somewhere—its number of views probably in the multi-millions by now, and likely to get another bump over the next week if Abe was hooked into the local gossip network. Still, Gray hoped the revelation bought him a little street cred.

"So, cop to cop, you can tell me. What's up with Dawn?"

Abe hesitated just a moment longer, then relented. Gray wasn't surprised. The man had to be lonely, without any colleagues in town he could talk to, face to face. "Dawn's been arrested," the other man admitted, obviously feeling conflicted about it.

"Arrested!" Gray blurted. "For what?" But as soon as he asked the question, he realized there could only be one reason.

Abe glanced left and right to confirm there was still no one else in earshot on this darkened dirt road in U-Turn, Alaska. He lowered his voice anyway.

"For *murder*," he hissed. "On orders from HQ, I arrested Dawn Atiqtalik Simmonds just after noon today for the murder of David Aġviq Simmonds, her brother."

Gazing into Abe Kanayurak's troubled eyes, Gray thought long and hard about this—Dawn, a murderer?—and decided he simply didn't believe it. He didn't know Dawn well, but she *was* a bright spot in this little community. No matter the brokenness of the woman's relationship with her brother, Gray couldn't believe she would have murdered him *or* anyone else. Not and continue to shine so brightly. "You must be mistaken," he told the other man.

Abe stiffened.

"Sorry," Gray said, immediately gesturing apologetically. "Of course you had to arrest her if you have probable cause. But..."

"But I have a hard time believing it too," Abe admitted, his shoulders slumping.

"Dawn is still here in U-Turn?" Gray asked.

"Yesss," Abe said slowly. "Over at my NSBPD substation."

Gray nodded thoughtfully. "I'd like to speak to her," he found himself saying.

"Um, no," Abe said flatly.

Gray blinked. But then, what was he expecting? There was only so far collegial regard would get him; he *was* now a private citizen, and well outside his original jurisdiction. Gray knew as well as anyone that suspects in police custody could receive visits only from certain authorized individuals. Personal visits weren't allowed until transfer to an actual jail—which in North Slope Borough probably meant transport to Utqiaġvik.

"Um, please?" Gray asked lamely, thinking furiously and coming up with nothing.

"Not unless you're her lawyer," Abe said drily. He sighed. "C'mon, man. Cop to cop, do you want to get me in trouble?"

Gray hung his head. Why *was* he trying so hard? He had no personal relationship with Dawn; and he certainly had no professional interest in any murder investigation, because it was no longer his profession. Quite simply, he had no stake in this matter. "When is she being transferred?" he asked.

Abe glanced at his watch before catching himself. "That information is not public. Look, Gaynes, if you really care this much, call HQ in Utqiaġvik. But I can't help you any further. I'm sorry." And with that, the cop spun on his heel and crunched away across the filthy permafrost road.

Gray wasn't paying attention anymore anyway. Abe had checked his watch when asked about Dawn's transfer, which meant it was happening today—likely in a matter of hours.

That didn't give Gray much time.

Two hours later, Gray stomped up the aluminum entrance ramp to the local NSBPD substation. It was a modular on stilts, just like all the neighboring buildings, and a small one at that. The fact that U-Turn had a police station at all was a testament to the size of TrephOil's operation here. To Gray's knowledge, the only other North Slope workcamp with a substation was Deadhorse in Prudhoe Bay, over a hundred miles to the east—and it housed as many as three *thousand* workers employed by multiple oil and gas operations.

With a deep breath, Gray rapped on the door, as sharply as he could manage with gloved knuckles.

Abe Kanayurak did not look pleased to see him. "Gaynes, I told you—"

Gray quickly held up a gallon-size plastic baggie. "Just dropping off some essential items for her." That *was* permitted, though it was arguable how essential any of the items truly was. Still, these were indeed Dawn's things, which her employee Ephron had helped Gray assemble at Dawn's house.

Frowning, Abe took the bag and turned it to examine the contents: three prescription pill bottles, a pair of reading glasses, and a printout containing several names and phone numbers—every defense attorney Gray could find with offices in North Slope Borough. There was also a business card stapled to that sheet, though Abe clearly didn't notice it.

"Fine," the cop said politely. "Thank you for your thoughtfulness. Good day." And he shut the door firmly in Gray's face.

Gray waited, pulling his balaclava back over his mouth and hugging himself. It took longer than it should have, but Abe eventually wrenched the door back open again. Wedging himself in the opening so Gray wouldn't see this as an invitation to enter, the cop held up the business card. It was plain white cardstock, relatively flimsy, and it read:

Grayson Gaynes
Private Investigator

With a start, Gray realized he hadn't even listed a phone number. He'd been in too much of a hurry 'designing' and sending the file to Dawn's aging inkjet. Still, it served its purpose.

"So you're a P.I. now?" Abe asked, with almost as much skepticism as he'd shown before, when Gray claimed a background with the NYPD.

"I am."

"Since when?"

"Oh, about twenty minutes ago," Gray said mildly, unzipping his parka to produce a manila folder. "I filed for a business license online, and the great state of Alaska doesn't require any special licensing for private investigators. Only if—"

"Only if you operate in Anchorage or Fairbanks," Abe finished for him. "I'm aware. And this?" He flipped Gray's lame business card around to show the note he had scribbled to Dawn there. "Telling her to represent herself until such time as a lawyer is appointed, then hiring you onto the defense team and instructing you to interview the 'suspect,' i.e. herself? Clever, Gaynes. A bit weak, legally speaking, but clever." Annoyed though he seemed, there was a small smile on Abe's lips.

"Look, officer," Gray said, deciding to be extra respectful. "I'm not trying to play games here. I just want to make sure Dawn gets a fair shake. I know you do too."

"I do," Abe admitted with a nod, "so I'm going to let you see her. But don't push your luck. Let her do most of the talking. If I feel like you're giving her advice, muddying matters or interfering with the case at all, then I will ask you to leave."

Gray raised his hands in surrender. "Thank you," he said genuinely.

"Come on, then. Get out of the cold already."

Gray eagerly complied, stepping inside and pulling fabric booties over his work boots. He had already scraped off the worst of the mud while waiting. Hanging his gloves and trapper hat by the door to dry, he followed Abe through the tiny modular building that served as the local police station. There were two narrow doors along one wall—probably a bathroom and a storage closet—then Abe's institutional metal desk. Rounding that, they turned down a short hallway to reach the substation's single small holding cell. It was all very Barney Fife. The cell wasn't even meant for holding true criminals, just the occasional disorderly conduct—a place for hot-tempered oil field workers to cool off after the rare fight broke out. Either way, it certainly wasn't a place for Dawn Simmonds.

"Gray!" cried her familiar voice when he came within sight. Even now, he detected some hint of her usual optimism, but it was severely strained. "Gray, they think I killed David!"

Gray looked through the steel bars—actual bars!—at the woman's familiar tattoos, the stripes on her chin and the V on her forehead. This was Dawn, alright, gazing out at him as brightly and hopefully as he had ever seen. "I heard," he said.

"And you're a private investigator?" she persisted. "You can help me prove I'm innocent?"

"I'm available to assist with your case, yes," he said carefully.

She saw right through it, of course, narrowing her eyes. "*You* don't think I killed him, do you?"

Of course he didn't. He wouldn't be here if he did, but... that was just an emotional opinion. If he was going to help Dawn, he needed to start thinking analytically, like the investigator he'd once been. "I know almost nothing about the case. Why don't you tell me what happened?"

She nodded, started pacing the cell, five steps one direction and five steps back. "I went to Nuiqsut to... identify David." Her eyes glistened. "But he was already gone. They had flown his... remains... to Anchorage for a real autopsy."

Abe was leaning against the wall nearby, of course, monitoring this conversation very carefully. He nodded confirmation.

Dawn swallowed a little convulsively and went on. "So mostly I met with the elders. Making arrangements, planning the service. It..." She examined her hands, rubbed at one of them. "It's more expensive than I realized. The village offered to help."

"Not unusual," Abe volunteered. "It *is* expensive. And in a case like this, the family would usually need to pay for transport of the body to and from Anchorage too. Assuming..." Assuming it wasn't the family who had murdered the man, he stopped himself from saying out loud.

Dawn took a breath. "Anyway, I drove back here this morning. Got ready for the evening meal crowd." She looked up finally, gave Gray a tremulous smile. "Wouldn't have minded taking another day off, but with all the bills about to start coming in, I couldn't afford to. Except..." Her eyes cut to Abe.

"Except Abe appeared at your door with an arrest warrant," Gray finished her sentence. "Why do the arrest here in U-Turn, though? Why not in Nuiqsut?" he asked, pronouncing the Iñupiaq village name carefully and mostly getting it right. "You were there for days, and that's where the case is being investigated, right?"

Abe shrugged. "The warrant wasn't issued until noon." He hesitated, then shrugged again. "Based on what evidence, they haven't yet told me."

Gray turned back to Dawn. "You say you drove back to U-Turn this morning. In your pickup?"

"Goodness, no!" she replied, for a moment sounding genuinely amused. "On my snow machine." She meant her snowmobile, of course, but none of the locals called them that. Gray should have known. All the Iñupiat had them, and in winter, they were the preferred method of transportation—capable of better speeds then pickup trucks and not constrained to the carefully-constructed snow roads.

Even after three seasons on the North Slope, Gray still forgot just how different this place was from everywhere else on the planet. It might as well be an alien world sometimes... if alien worlds had monster bears that meandered through town, occasionally attacking and even eating people.

"Why *did* the NSBPD stop thinking David was killed by that bear?" he asked. Maybe there was something in the man's remains indicating he'd been dead long before his body was eaten? But that still left a lot of other possibilities, accidental death generally the most plausible of them. Gray glanced back and forth between Dawn and Abe. "Does either of you know what evidence was found to suggest murder? Either by Dawn or anyone else?"

Dawn shook her head emphatically. Abe, probably realizing he shouldn't be so honest about knowing so little, said, "I have no such information to release at this time."

Gray sighed. "Tell me about the last time you saw David alive," he asked Dawn, then immediately forestalled her response. "Recognize that you are not entitled to confidentiality when talking to me, because I'm not a lawyer. Abe is here in an official capacity, and he's dutybound to report everything you say—and it can and will be used against you in court, just like he told you before." Gray hesitated. "Abe *did* read you your rights, correct? Your Miranda warning?"

Dawn nodded, Abe looking mildly offended.

"Good," Gray continued. "So if you have anything to say that might be misconstrued as even vaguely incriminating, don't. Wait and share that with your defense attorney instead, once you hire one." He glanced at Abe again, worried the man might see even this warning as interference in the case, but the cop simply nodded.

"It's okay," Dawn assured them both. "I have nothing to hide."

"Good. So the last time you saw David... Where was it, what did you discuss...?"

"Gosh, I don't even know when that was," Dawn admitted, obviously embarrassed. "It might have been last summer, more than a year ago."

Gray froze. That wasn't what she'd told Abe the other night at the bar, a discrepancy Abe immediately noticed too. "You told me you saw David in September," the cop said darkly. "Just three months ago, before he motored south for the winter."

Dawn waved a hand easily. "No, September's the last time I *spoke* with him. Assuming a text message counts as speaking. But I didn't actually *see* him." Her expression darkened again, the ugly version of Dawn that Gray had observed for the first time the other night when discussing her brother—but twisted, conflicted now that he was dead. "Check my phone; I never delete texts. He sent me a message, said he wanted to clear the air. David *asked* me to meet him in person, but he never showed."

"Meet him where?" Gray had his phone out now, tilted to show Abe he was in a note-taking app, not recording or doing anything else the NSBPD might disapprove of.

"On his boat, the *Bowhead II*," Dawn sneered. "Maybe twenty-five or thirty miles offshore."

Gray blinked. "Offshore? Not in Nuiqsut, or even Utqiaġvik?"

"Have you *seen* his boat?" she scoffed.

Gray glanced at Abe and back to Dawn. "Why would I have seen his boat?" he asked dumbly.

"Because *everyone*'s seen it," she said angrily. "Monstrous, ugly thing." She waved a hand. "Okay, not ugly. It's sleek, beautiful, but... it just doesn't *belong* up here. You've seen the sorta boats we drive in the summer. No? Mostly 16-to-24-foot river boats, jetted—no props—for a six-inch draft. The biggest boats our hunters use are 30-foot cabin cruisers."

Abe was nodding agreement.

"My brother..." Dawn scoffed. "His boat is *twice* that size, with a five-foot draft—meaning the water needs to be at *least* five feet deep to accommodate it. That boat's completely useless for inland navigation."

"And this offended you?" Gray asked slowly. Clearly he was still missing something.

"That offended everyone!" Dawn said. She sighed. "It wasn't so much the boat as what it represented—the message David was sending by bringing it around." She abruptly sat on one of the cell's two cots. "David always thought he was better than the rest of us, you see? He went off to Anchorage for college. Not that unusual. Then Fairbanks for his PhD in marine biology, and we fully supported that too; because his studies honored his heritage, his connection to the land and *all* its inhabitants, not just the people. But then he got awarded a big time research grant and he was swimming in money, and he just had to rub our noses in it—had to show everyone he'd *outgrown* his heritage."

"How so?" Gray asked, to keep her talking. He still didn't understand the depth of her vehemence; but then, this wasn't his culture. On the other hand, family was often unfair in its expectations, no matter the culture. "What exactly did he do that was offensive, and who else did he offend?"

"It began when he got that grant, maybe... five or six years back? The start of that summer, David anchored the *Bowhead* as close to Utqiaġvik as possible and immediately started showing it off."

"Again, he didn't dock *at* Utqiaġvik?" Gray asked.

Abe spoke up. "Not even Utqiaġvik can accommodate a boat that size. It doesn't have any deepwater ports, because Iñupiat boats are all beach-launched."

"But that wasn't a problem for David," Dawn said. "His boat was so big it carried another, smaller motorboat onboard. So he came ashore in that, and immediately started ferrying his friends back and forth. He was actually giving *tours*, so everyone could see his high-tech equipment, his plush cabins. I get it; he needed a big ocean-going vessel for his research. That's fine. But he didn't buy just any seaworthy ship. He splurged on the biggest, nicest, flashiest yacht he could find, then had it customized with all the bells and whistles—and began strutting it like some sort of status symbol." She took a deep breath, but it didn't calm her. "And even after folks stopped going out to see it, his behavior continued. He would bring his launch into Utqiaġvik far more than necessary, throwing money around on frivolous things. Eating out, actually bragging about his life. Just *having* store-bought gear is a form of bragging for our people, much less talking about it, and he repeatedly purchased more stuff that he didn't need. It didn't take long for folks to start shunning him. So the next summer, when he showed up again, he brought a bunch of expensive gifts from overseas—and he started trying to buy goodwill."

Gray was frowning. None of this behavior struck him as offensive so much as immature. David Simmonds sounded like a young man who wanted to impress others, to be liked. He just went about it in a childish way. As for his spending habits... "You're sure he wasn't just trying to stimulate the economy? Share the blessings of the wealth he'd been granted?"

Dawn's eyes flashed, and Gray leaned back involuntarily. "That is not the way of my people.

Calling attention to yourself, *talking* about yourself, it's taboo."

Abe nodded.

"And our economy does *not* need stimulation," she added firmly.

"Okay," Gray said, hands raised. He was starting to understand, at least a little. Whatever the young man's intentions, David Simmonds' actions were apparently very offensive to other Native Alaskans. But in terms of Dawn's defense, that was good. It meant there were potentially *many* other individuals with hard feelings toward the victim. "Wait, though," Gray said. "Fast forward to this year again—September, when he texted you. If David had a motorboat launch, why did he want to meet you offshore? He could've easily met you in Utqiaġvik. From everything you just told me, he came ashore all the time."

Dawn sighed. "He said he wanted to show me something on the *Bowhead.* Something specific, though he probably just wanted to give me the same tour as everyone else. I'd always refused before. Still... he said he wanted to apologize for everything. So..." She shrugged. "So he sent me coordinates, and against my better judgment, I took my own cabin cruiser out to meet him." She sagged. "But like I say, he never showed. I waited almost an hour before giving up and coming home."

Gray was frowning. "And how big is your cabin cruiser?"

"Normal size. 20-footer."

"You took a 20-foot boat thirty miles offshore?"

"Sure. Why not?"

Abe didn't seem to think this was odd either. "On a nice day, you can go out fifty, maybe a hundred miles," the cop assured him. "Depending on ice and winds."

Gray shook his head. Alien world indeed. "Um..." He tried to collect his thoughts. "What was the grant for? What was David researching?"

"Whale migration patterns," Dawn said with a wave of her hand. "Took him as far south as Central America in the winter. Yet another thing he bragged about often."

"And his grant was that generous?" Gray asked, finally picking at something that had been bothering him. "Not only to pay for his yacht and supplies—that much makes sense, being directly related to his research—but with enough left over to live so flamboyantly?"

"Apparently," Dawn said, putting her face in her hands and groaning. "I asked him the same thing once, and he just said it was from a private institute. More money, less strings attached." She looked up. "Look, Gray... why does any of this matter to my case?"

"I'm not sure it does," Gray admitted. This *had* turned into a bit of a tangent. "At this stage, it's hard to say which details have bearing on a case, so it's best to just find out as much as I can." He glanced over his notes. "Tell me about David's wristwatch. It must be rather unique if authorities made a tentative ID of David's remains based solely on the watch."

Dawn was pacing again. "Oh, it was unique alright. Solid gold with actual diamonds instead of numbers—at least he insisted they were real, the braggart. It was a gaudy thing."

Gray was tapping rapidly. "What brand?"

She shrugged, but Abe was at his desk, going through a file. "There's no harm showing you this," he said, returning to hand Gray the glossy 8x10 from the other night. "It's essentially public knowledge."

Gray felt his eyebrows rise when he saw the logo emblazoned on the watch face. He did a quick Internet search on his phone. "Some of these watches sell for a hundred thousand dollars!"

"Like I say. Gaudy," Dawn concluded disgustedly. She didn't seem remotely impressed by the price tag, though it was probably twice what she earned in a whole year.

Gray spent another couple minutes online, satisfying himself that David's wristwatch probably *was* authentic. Only a pure gold watchband and a sapphire crystal face would have resisted the acid in a bear's stomach for any period of time.

"So," Gray concluded finally. "Everything about David was offensive, from his boat to his watch to his behavior."

With a sigh, Dawn seated herself again. "Yeah. He's..." She stopped herself, switched to past tense. "He alienated pretty much everyone before the end."

"Can you think of anyone in particular who may have wanted to harm him as a result?" Gray asked carefully.

Dawn sagged. She thought for a moment, but ultimately shook her head. "He was disliked, maybe even hated. But to kill him because of it? No," she said honestly. "I can't think of anyone who felt *that* way about him. It goes entirely against our culture. David was a lost soul. He engendered a lot of hard feelings, but a lot of pity as well."

Gray took her word for it, tapping his notes. Still, *someone* had killed David Simmonds. Maybe no one else had motive for premeditated murder, but maybe someone—other than Dawn—had killed the man in anger. Certainly the man hadn't been robbed, if he was left with that watch strapped to his wrist. Of course, such a watch would have been too unique to safely pawn.

Unfortunately, since Dawn stood to inherit that same wristwatch, the watch all by itself provided plausible motive for *her* to commit the murder. Especially on top of all the hard feelings.

There was still far too much Gray didn't know about this case, starting with the evidence leading to Dawn's arrest. But at almost 7 p.m., he *did* finally have a chance to ask someone who knew—because that was when two NSBPD detectives arrived from Utqiaġvik to take Dawn into custody.

They weren't much pleased to find Gray there, talking with their suspect, but they were professional enough as they put an end to it. One of the detectives escorted Gray to the door as the other filled out paperwork with Abe, taking possession of Dawn's holstered revolver along with the gallon-sized baggie of medication and essentials.

Gray finally posed the all-important question when they were out of Dawn's hearing. "At least tell me this much," Gray said as he—slowly as possible—put on his hat and gloves. "How do you know David Simmonds was murdered by another human being? And what evidence do you have that Dawn committed the crime?"

The detective eyed Gray for a long moment. A name bar pinned to his NSBPD uniform shirt gave his surname as JAMESON, but it was the man's short blond hair that gave him away as tunnuq like Gray. "How do we know?" he repeated finally.

Gray nodded, eager to hear the answer.

"We know because the victim said so. David Simmonds himself identified his sister as his murderer."

And before Gray could think of a response to *that*, he was being pushed back out into the cold.

The next week, December 11 - 19th

North Slope Borough

Gray spent the next hour pondering that statement, trying to make sense of it. How could David Simmonds have named his killer? As in literally how, by what practical mechanism, could he have done such a thing? A message sent prior to his murder, expressing suspicion that his sister was out to get him? A voicemail left after he'd been mortally wounded, but was still clinging to life? Something else? For that matter, when had this communication occurred? When had the *murder* occurred? It might have happened anytime between September and last week, based on the information Gray had gathered so far—which was far too little information to theorize about anything, truthfully, but that didn't stop his brain from turning it over and over.

In his rush to help Dawn, gathering her essentials and registering his new P.I. business, Gray had entirely lost track of time. His work shift had started an hour ago, and he had missed the bus to his drilling site. So his next stop was the motor pool, where he filled out the form to requisition a work truck.

He continued to ponder what little he knew of David and Dawn Simmonds as he waited on the keys. He pondered as he trudged from there to the cafeteria to hastily pack his lunch. And he pondered for the entirety of his thirty-minute, 20 mph drive to the work site.

He *stopped* pondering upon arrival, when Toolpusher Tim ripped into him for his tardiness. The man's anger was real and it was fair, for—starting this season—Gray now filled a critical role. Whereas the crew could have made do without one of the roustabouts, the nonappearance of a roughneck had required the bus to wait until a substitute could be found from one of the morning shifts, which had cost them half an hour. In short, *everyone* was miffed with Gray as he took his place on the drill floor, trading places with the substitute, who took the work truck back to camp. Tim made loud and clear that there would be a notation on Gray's record. Since any recurrence of the problem would likely result in termination, Gray threw himself into the work without complaint, resolving to avoid even the hint of a bad attitude in the near future. He liked this job too much to risk losing it. In short, he was so totally focused on work that he had no more time to think about David Simmonds.

But he didn't stop worrying about Dawn, a feeling of unease that never went away.

After that shift ended Tuesday morning, he learned that the two NSBPD detectives had bundled Dawn off to U-Turn's small airstrip, flying from there to Utqiaġvik aboard one of the NSB Search & Rescue prop planes that doubled as police transport when necessary.

And that was the last Gray heard of Dawn that week.

Abe refused to tell him anything in the days that followed. Even the rumor mill seemed completely in the dark. Gray kept expecting to get a phone call from an Utqiaġvik defense attorney, but that still hadn't happened by the time his Thursday shift began. (Dammit, why hadn't he at least *hand*written his cell phone number on that new business card of his?) So Friday—during the midday hours, when he should have been sleeping—Gray gamely started calling each of the attorneys on the list he had given Dawn; but none could or would give him answers either. If one of them had taken Dawn's case, confidentiality prevented him from saying so without her permission... which she'd apparently not given. Was that an oversight? Had Dawn even hired a lawyer yet?

Meanwhile, Gray still had a job to do. So he worked out the rest of the hitch, his second week coming to an end the following Tuesday morning. But the moment he boarded the bus for the trip back to U-Turn, Gray's mind switched gears again.

All the guys started showering, packing, stripping beds when they got back to the dorms—and all of it in surly silence, as was normal at the end of a hitch. Even Motormouth Miller knew not to risk too much humor at this point. Gray followed form, staying as inconspicuous as possible, lest he draw any lingering wrath from his fellows after his tardiness last week.

At last, they boarded another bus for their own short run to the airstrip. There, they and all the other workers going off-hitch huddled in plastic seats at the terminal, awaiting the appearance of the plane that would take them home to Anchorage. It had been a long two weeks, as usual. Fourteen straight days of twelve-hour shifts for each man (and the occasional woman)—84 hours each week, the first 40 paid at their contractual hourly rate, the remaining 44 at time-and-a-half. All that overtime had bought each sloper two weeks completely off work, starting now. But no one was smiling. An eerie quiet pervaded the small terminal, punctuated only by terse grunts or muttered communication with the gate agent.

Then came the arrival of the Alaska Airlines Boeing 737, and men immediately began sitting up straighter. Compared with everything they had endured over the last half month, the jetliner's landing was just so... normal. It touched down lightly in the midday twilight, taxiing toward them along the runway—the largest stretch of asphalt to be found for a hundred miles in any direction. Soon thereafter the gate opened, and the terminal was filled with the laughter of men freshly rested, those coming to replace Gray and his compatriots.

Gray allowed himself a smile. Soon his work crew would be winging home. Somewhere about halfway back, Miller would offer a tentative wisecrack. There would be more wan smiles, some tired laughter—a general thawing as the guys saw sunlight again through their cabin windows. Even Gray, despite his day blindness, usually enjoyed that moment. He would lean back against the headrest, eyes closed, and simply bask in the sun's radiant warmth.

But Gray wouldn't be there to see it this time.

He slipped away to the restroom to avoid awkward questions, then reappeared once the outbound flight had boarded—a process that went with practiced ease, far more quickly than most commercial flights. He stepped to the window to watch taxi and takeoff, the exhausted part of him very much wishing he was on his way home too. Instead, he pulled out his cell phone and tossed off a quick text message to his father, making him aware that he would *not* need a ride from the Anchorage airport.

Then he stepped over to the counter to speak with the gate agent once more. "Two hours from now," she told him brightly, in answer to his question.

Stifling a sigh, Gray thanked her and wandered toward the vending machines.

He had canceled his flight home yesterday morning, but not before making alternate arrangements. Gray had called around to all the companies that operated bush planes in North Slope Borough, asking if there were any flights already going through U-Turn today. He had eventually found an open seat on one of the planes the U.S. Postal Service chartered for mail delivery to NSB's remote villages and work camps.

That plane proved to be a Cessna 185, which its pilot described as "the airborne version of a four-wheel-drive, three-quarter-ton pickup truck." Indeed, the little bush plane bounced like one too. Having offloaded U-Turn's plastic postal tote and welcomed Gray aboard, the pilot put the plane through a quick turn and shoved the large red throttle lever forward. The sudden acceleration shoved Gray back in his seat, and he wondered yet again why he was going to so much trouble for a woman he barely knew. Thumbing a ride on this little six-seater, over arctic tundra no less, was definitely *not* normal. And yet he couldn't help watching the pilot's practiced motions with keen interest. Gray certainly had a good vantage, folded into the seat right next to the man.

Eventually, Gray grew accustomed to the loud, bumpy flight. The friendly garrulousness of the pilot helped, as he kept up a steady stream of conversation over the headset. Introducing himself as Jacob, he explained that he didn't usually have passengers but always enjoyed the company when he did. He was full of questions for Gray about TrephOil and what it was like to be a roughneck, living in a work camp largely devoid of women and children. Jacob himself was happily married, his wife and four children awaiting him in Utqiaġvik, where Jacob's little Cessna was due to land tonight.

First, though, they had stops to make in Nuiqsut and Atqasuk. It barely seemed they had reached altitude out of U-Turn before they were landing again in Dawn's hometown. Touchdown in Nuiqsut was a little harrowing for Gray, a big-city New Yorker who had never heard of—much less experienced—a gravel airstrip before; but Jacob explained this was nothing compared to coming down hard on snowpack using *ski* landing gear. Gray decided he would take the man's word for it.

Back in the air again a short time later, the two men talked of murder—for the recently discovered murder of David Aġviq Simmonds was now common knowledge, especially in Nuiqsut, where the necropsy of the bear had first uncovered his remains. *Why* the police suspected foul play was still a mystery to the average joe, but not the fact of it; and here in North Slope Borough, murder was a big deal. Gray had already researched the numbers. Whereas his home borough of Manhattan 'boasted' hundreds of murders every year, NSB went many years with none at all, and seldom more than one or two. Of course, despite the fact that its territory stretched almost 100,000 square miles, it had barely a tenth that many inhabitants. It was only natural that the murder of one of those individuals, no matter how disliked or how seasonal his presence, would be cause for great concern.

Gray didn't tell Jacob that he himself knew the accused murderer, aside from admitting he'd eaten at her establishment on occasion. However, when they landed at Atqasuk an hour after Nuiqsut, Gray stayed in the suddenly quiet cockpit while Jacob unloaded. He seized the opportunity to make calls to his list of lawyers once more. It would be too late to call when the Cessna finally landed in Utqiaġvik, hours after close of business; and Gray wanted to reiterate that *if* one of those attorneys had taken Dawn's case, Gray was eager to join the defense team. Not only was he an experienced investigator; he was a personal acquaintance of Dawn's who had already spoken with her at length about the case.

Gray relayed this first to one gracious lawyer, then to another less patient man who asked him to stop calling. His third call of the day, to an attorney named Leavitt, finally bore fruit. Mr. Leavitt was now permitted to say that Dawn was his client and had granted consent to discuss matters with Gray. Leavitt was surprised and cautiously pleased to hear that Gray would be visiting his office first thing in the morning.

As the Cessna embarked on the final leg toward Utqiaġvik, its pilot chattering pleasantly once more, Gray was finally able to relax. It had been a long two-week hitch, and an especially tiring last day of that hitch. He hadn't slept in more than 24 hours, aside from a catnap in the airport; and in that time, he'd constantly second-guessed this decision to fly to Utqiaġvik despite no official invitation to join the defense team. Now he could finally put those worries to rest. For good or ill, he was on Dawn's team now.

For the entirety of his short career as an NYPD detective, Gray Gaynes had worked to put killers behind bars, developing a reputation within the homicide squad as an intuitive—if overly-methodical at times—investigator. But now, after a seven-year hiatus, he was going to turn all that on its head. Instead of building a case to convict, he would build a case to acquit. At least, he would follow the facts of the case wherever they led; but if they went where he expected, then he would do everything in his power to clear this woman's name.

Gray's eyes fluttered closed, and he slept most of the remaining distance to Utqiaġvik, drawing a smile from Jacob when the pilot finally noticed. And despite the bumpy touchdown of yet another landing on gravel, Gray didn't even stir until Jacob quietly shook him awake.

"Mr. Gaynes? We've arrived."

Wednesday, December 20th
Utqiaġvik

Utqiaġvik—formerly known as Barrow—was the seat of government in the North Slope Borough of Alaska, which encompassed almost all U.S. territory above the Arctic Circle. It still boggled Gray's mind that this entire swath of land, nearly 100,000 square miles of it, had the equivalent of a county government. But then, its 11,000 inhabitants were spread across a mere eight villages and various oil company work camps. As home to half of those people all by itself, Utqiaġvik was the largest NSB settlement by far.

Naturally, that made it the headquarters for the police department too, as well as the place Dawn was being held awaiting trial. Yet Gray's first visit wouldn't be to her, but to her new attorney.

The former New Yorker had easily found lodging at one of several inns the night before. After a quick breakfast, he set out for the day, walking an icy street under the persistent night sky. The town had a rustic beauty, despite the utter dearth of foliage. Many of the snow-topped clapboard buildings were painted vibrantly and strewn with Christmas decorations, appearing festive even to Gray's color-blind eyes. Yes, it was that time of the year again; it always was, when Gray returned to the North Slope for the start of a new drilling season. But decorated or not, this town felt so much more real, more human than U-Turn, though the structures here too were built on stilts to keep them out of the snow-caked permafrost. Even the utilities, including the water and sewer pipes, ran largely aboveground for the same reason—all of it lit by streetlights and aurora borealis.

Still, the subzero temps made this an austere place no matter how the locals tried to brighten the landscape. Gray should have been waking in his own bed in Anchorage right now, the rays of a real sunrise peeking through the blinds. Instead, he was trudging along another unpaved road, the next sunrise in these parts still a month away, at risk of losing fingers or toes to frostbite. Despite everything, he had to laugh.

There were no Ubers in Utqiaġvik, but Gray didn't make it fifty yards before the first passing motorist offered him a ride. He accepted gratefully, hopping into the cab of the pickup truck with its gracious owner.

The law offices of S. Taluġnaitchuk Leavitt were housed in yet another clapboard building with a ramp leading to its front door. Gray knocked and was quickly ushered inside the small suite by the paralegal, a young woman with tattoos like Dawn's but distinct—the same V on the forehead, but different shapes on the cheeks, a different number of lines on her chin. She soon introduced him to Mr. Leavitt, the practice's only other employee. He was a tall, brawny man with a friendly smile and kind eyes. Though obviously Iñupiaq as well, based on his name, nothing about the man's appearance set him apart as Native Alaskan. Gray had learned to expect that. It was primarily today's young women who chose the traditional markings, reclaiming some of the cultural heritage that was almost lost over the last hundred years. Aside from body art, Iñupiat were often indistinguishable from those of outside origin (though anyone with blond or auburn hair, or skin tone especially light or dark, was obviously tunnuq). And the locals were so hospitable, they didn't seem to care about such distinctions anyway.

Mr. Leavitt was no exception. Seizing Gray's hand in an iron grip, he insisted on being addressed by his first name, Samuel, despite the way his signboard read. Gray insisted on the same informality; Samuel had him sign some paperwork; and they quickly got down to business.

"First off, you should know that bail was denied," Samuel said as he poured coffee for all three of them, including his paralegal Esther. "Due to severity of the crime and flight risk."

"Dawn's a flight risk?" Gray questioned in some surprise. "Her entire life is here. She's never even left the North Slope, has she?"

Samuel snorted, setting a mug before Gray on the big conference room table. "The North Slope is largely uninhabited, untold miles of emptiness. If someone wanted to flee the villages and hide in the wilderness, it would be a monster of a task trying to find them."

"But how would they survive outside in these temperatures?" Gray asked, blowing on the steaming coffee to cool it.

"Oh, they wouldn't have to live outside. Most Iñupiat families have private allotments of land, hunting or fishing camps we retreat to whenever we want to get away from this urban hustle and bustle." His eyes twinkled and Gray laughed.

Esther spoke up. "My family has a reindeer herding station. I was practically raised there. We have a gas power generator and everything."

"But most such camps are boarded up in winter," Samuel concluded. "So you see, if someone *did* go on the run, there would be plenty of places to hide until the thaw—after which escape by boat would be easy, considering the abundance of waterways. Hence, bail was denied." He sighed. "And Gray, I have to tell you, bail would've been a long shot anyway. Based on the facts of the case, it doesn't look good for our client."

"And yet you seem pretty eager to work this case," Esther observed to Gray, sipping from her mug. "Do you actually think Dawn Simmonds is innocent?"

Gray nodded. "I do, provisionally. Based on my experience interviewing suspects, seeing how guilty people respond to accusations." He finally took a sip of his own coffee and scalded his tongue. "It's not that Dawn's incapable of murder. Everyone is capable. But... I don't think a person like Dawn could commit such an act without being fundamentally changed."

Samuel and Esther traded a look, so Gray hurried to explain.

"Murdering another human being, it leaves an indelible mark on your soul. And I think Dawn is too free and joyful a person to be hiding such a scar." Gray didn't say that he was less confident in his instincts than in past years. He had been too thoroughly deceived during the Mad Batter investigation to ever be *over*confident again. He cocked his head at the other two members of Dawn's defense team. "You sound like you *don't* believe she's innocent?"

"Well, we don't know her as well as you..." Samuel began diplomatically.

Gray snorted. "I confess I don't really know her that well myself. We've just been acquainted for a few years, our interactions regular but surface-level. My read could be off," he admitted.

Samuel nodded, grateful for the clarification. "But you're willing to give her the benefit of the doubt. As the law demands all of us do."

"Exactly."

"Good." The lawyer took a deep breath. "Professionally, I am committed to aggressively defending my client's interests, regardless of my personal feelings. However... it may be in her best interests to take a plea deal, based on the evidence uncovered so far."

Gray straightened, setting down the coffee mug. "Tell me."

Samuel started flipping through one of his many legal pads. "As soon as the police had tentative ID on the murder victim's remains—something Dawn herself assisted with, by confirming that was David's wristwatch—the NSBPD filed a warrant for access to David's cloud storage. I'm not sure if you're aware, but he was a marine biologist who lived on his boat. There had been no reported sightings of the man *or* that boat for months, and everyone assumed he had followed his usual pattern of motoring south for the winter. Obviously, we now know that he didn't. With their warrant, the police were hoping to track David's phone, to um... find the rest of his remains."

Gray glanced between Samuel and Esther. "You're saying they found only partial human remains in the bear's stomach?" he clarified. He had wondered about this for weeks, because it seemed unlikely even the biggest bear could consume an entire adult human all at once.

Samuel looked queasy. "There was most of an arm inside that bear, including the small bones of the left hand largely intact—still wearing that gold wristwatch." He shook his head. "All partially digested, of course, which is why fingerprinting was impossible."

"But *only* an arm?" Gray pressed excitedly. "Meaning David Simmonds could still be alive?"

"No," Samuel said, sadly but confidently. "Neither cell nor satellite service providers could ping David's phone; its battery probably died long ago. But... certain files in the man's cloud storage leave little doubt as to what actually happened to him."

"I don't understand," Gray said. "When you say cloud storage, I assume you're talking about computer files backed up on the Internet? What files?"

"Videos. As a biologist, it appears David Simmonds filed video log entries every few days. It was his way of documenting findings and theories for future reference."

Something clicked for Gray. "So *that's* how he implicated Dawn. On one of these videos? The NSBPD detective I met—Jameson—said David himself named Dawn as his killer."

Samuel nodded. He now had a laptop computer open in front of him, and he was clicking, pulling up a file.

"But how does that tell you exactly what happened to him?" Gray persisted.

"Just... watch the video for yourself," Samuel said. And with that, he spun the laptop screen to face Gray fully.

The video log entry was paused on its initial frame. The first thing Gray noticed was the face of the man centered in that frame—his wide eyes, the beads of sweat on his forehead. This was David Aġviq Simmonds, presumably, and he was scared. The second thing Gray noticed was the timestamp, superimposed on the image in the bottom-right corner: `2023-09-13T11:41:57+12`. In other words, September 13, 2023 at 11:41 a.m.—now over three months prior.

Eyes crawling carefully over every pixel of the freeze-frame, Gray sought out other meaningful details. The camera was pointed straight at David's face, shot from up close and slightly below the level of the man's eyes—likely a laptop webcam, then, built right into the top of the computer's screen. The positioning of David's hands, mostly out of frame at the bottom of the shot, suggested they were resting on the laptop's keyboard and/or trackpad mouse. The man was dressed in a long-sleeve shirt, but without headgear or gloves, and there was no indication from his cheeks or eyes that he'd been outside in the cold recently. A few feet behind David was a wall, a joint in that wall visible just over his right shoulder—a vertical seam where two panels were riveted together. Gray immediately recognized this as a bulkhead wall, of the sort found on a vessel, perhaps the victim's own yacht *Bowhead II.*

As usual, Gray saw all of this in black and white, thanks to his own unique perspective on the world.

He pressed 'play.'

Immediately, the sound of David's labored breathing filled the air, interrupted only by a single hard swallow as he sat back in his chair. Folding his hands in his lap, David stared wildly into the camera... and said nothing. Nervously, he glanced up and to the right—just over the edge of his laptop screen?—then back into the camera. He looked down, took a deep breath, then squinted yet again into the lens... and finally, it seemed, came to a decision.

"*I've just made the most awful discovery,*" he said hoarsely. He cleared his throat. "*It... This changes everything I thought I knew about what I'm doing out here. I just—*" He wiped his face, his courage seeming to waver. Then he took another deep breath and settled his shoulders. "*Hell with it. In case something happens to me, I want the truth to—*"

A sudden loud banging made Gray and David both jump in their seats, David looking up and to the right again, eyes wider than ever. It was the sound of a fist rapping emphatically, maybe angrily at a door. Then came a muffled voice, barely distinguishable as human, the words indiscernible.

"*No, everything is fine,*" David insisted in response. "*I'll be out in a moment.*" Then he leaned toward the camera with a determined expression, speaking in the faintest of whispers: "*I just found out that—*"

This time the interruption was even more violent, an awful thud and splintering as (Gray imagined) someone kicked in the door to David's cabin.

With a yelp, the young man leapt to his feet, almost tripping over his desk chair as he scrambled backwards. Standing now, his face was momentarily out of frame, reappearing only as he backpedaled into the bulkhead—his expression full of guilt. It was a facial reaction anyone would recognize, of a man caught in the act of doing something he shouldn't. For good measure, David's eyes flicked to the camera and back up again. "*It's not what it looks like,*" he tried to tell the intruder, who remained offscreen. Then the biologist's eyes popped wide in abject terror. "*Wait, Dawn, I'm begging you,* please! *Don't—*"

The end came quickly. Three strangely innocuous pops on the audio track, which Gray recognized only from experience—the sound of a gun discharging in close proximity to a cheap microphone, the sudden immense change in air pressure overwhelming the mic's ability to accurately capture the sound. Onscreen, two gaping holes appeared in David Simmonds' chest, and then the top half of his head simply ceased to exist—reappearing as a glistening spray of gore across the bulkhead wall.

Then came the sound of two quick footfalls, and the laptop was slammed violently shut, offering only a momentary glimpse of the computer's own keyboard before all went black. In that last dark frame, nothing but the final timestamp remained:

`2023-09-13T11:43:13+12`

The biologist's last log entry was less than a minute and a half long. A drab, colorless presentation of murder, like the gruesome slaying of an elderly couple in an elevator car eight and a half years prior—another homicide Gray had been forced to watch on video, his first case back on the job after his own wife's murder.

Gray fought off a rush of feeling. That had been a different lifetime. He needed to focus on the present. "That *was* David, I presume?" Obviously it was, but he asked to be sure.

"Yes," Samuel said simply. He and Esther had both rather pointedly looked elsewhere during Gray's review of the footage. Apparently they'd already seen it enough times for themselves.

Gray swallowed bile, finding it strangely reassuring that he could still experience such a visceral reaction after everything he'd faced in his career. He glanced at the video timestamp once more. "September. So David's been dead more than three months." He made a face, forcing down another wave of nausea. "His body would be in an advanced state of decomposition by now, and obviously the bear only recently found him. What would possess any animal to..."

Samuel was shaking his head. "Remember where we are. I doubt anywhere in the North Slope has gotten above freezing in the last three months."

Gray sighed. "You're right. Like keeping a body in the cooler at the morgue, preserved indefinitely. Do the police know yet *where* the bear found him?"

The lawyer shook his head again. "They're still working on that."

Gray sat back, thinking. Three months. Three *months* since the murder. He'd known that was a possibility, but it was on the very outside edge of the timeframe. Learning now that David Simmonds had really been murdered that long ago, he reexamined his assumptions. If Dawn had murdered her brother, that meant she'd had *two* whole months to learn to smile again before Gray even returned to NSB at the start of the season. Was he a fool for thinking he could see through her, if she really was the killer? Maybe.

He pointed thoughtfully at Samuel's laptop. "Do we know where Dawn was on that day—September 13—at that time?"

The big lawyer squirmed. "Yesss," he said slowly. "Best we can tell, she was on her own boat, some thirty miles out to sea... meeting up with the victim."

Gray had been afraid of that. "Dawn said David never showed up to that meeting."

Samuel shrugged. "She told me the same. Unfortunately, she also told the *police* already too." He pursed his lips. "And since she can't prove he never showed..."

"It looks bad," Gray agreed. "From their perspective, she already confessed to meeting with the victim on the day he was killed. What about the text message David sent her with the meeting location? Do the date and time match the murder?"

"No. Because there *was* no text exchange." Samuel scowled. "At least, if there was, she deleted it off her phone."

"Dawn said she never deletes texts." Gray thought a moment. "Did the phone delete it automatically, once it was more than a month old?"

Samuel just shook his head again. "No... because she still has history of older texts back and forth with her brother. Worse, *those* exchanges tend to be rather... contentious."

Gray sat back, surprised. Those texts would have told the police exactly where Dawn planned to be at the time of her brother's murder, either giving her an alibi or making her look even guiltier. Deleting such evidence was the act of a guilty person... and the way she'd apparently done so wasn't even very smart. Better by far if she'd simply changed her phone settings to expunge old messages automatically, providing a reasonable excuse why the messages were no longer available. But she hadn't done that.

"Yeah," Samuel said, reading the dismay on Gray's face. "Like I say, it looks pretty bad for her."

"But this is all still circumstantial," Gray said doggedly. "If Dawn was actually guilty, why even admit she was planning to meet with David?"

"Maybe she didn't know this video of his murder was preserved in the cloud?" Esther suggested. "Complete with timestamp?"

"What about GPS location data?" Gray asked. "For either David or Dawn on that day?"

"There's nothing in David's cloud storage." Samuel waved a hand. "Actually, there's a *lot* in his account. Tons of massive video logs and other technical data related to his research—but no GPS tracking. He apparently had location services turned off on his phone. If police can find his boat, maybe the onboard systems will shed more light... but that's something of a chicken-and-egg problem."

"And Dawn's phone?"

"Police have filed another warrant for *her* cloud backups. If her phone tracked her location that day, they'll get that history at the same time they recover any deleted texts. But that could take days." The big lawyer's shoulders slumped. "There's honestly not much we can do for her until then."

Gray massaged his temples, thinking. "Well, the easiest way to secure a suspect's release is to provide a more likely suspect."

Samuel barked a laugh. "You're forgetting one of the most damning bits of evidence. The victim himself spoke her name quite clearly. He said, and I quote: '*Wait! Dawn, I'm begging you. Please don't...*' and then BAM, he got shot."

The lawyer wasn't wrong. The sound and video quality of David's last entry was quite clear, and there was no arguing that he actually pronounced some other, similar-sounding name. Gray even re-wound and re-watched one more time, just to be sure. "But Dawn isn't that uncommon a name," Gray pointed out.

"It is up here," Samuel retorted. "A lot of Iñupiat first names are Biblical, thanks to the missionaries way back when. Not all of them—especially among kids these days, including my own—but I'm sure I've never known another Dawn. Not in NSB."

"And what about Donald?" Gray asked gamely. "Which can *also* be shortened to Don, D-O-N?" He hesitated. "Is that a Biblical name?"

From the look Samuel and Esther shared then, it was clear neither had considered David might be saying *Don*. "No, I don't think Donald is Biblical," Samuel said slowly, "but not everyone in North Slope is Iñupiaq. It's still not common, but yes, I *have* known a few D-O-N Dons. And there would have to be a few more in the oil company work camps too."

"Not common is actually a good thing," Gray said, perking up. An uncommon name in a community of only 11,000 souls... "It means fewer leads to chase down. All I need to do is look into each 'Don' in the North Slope and see if any of them had a beef with David Simmonds." Gray gestured to the computer. "Can you search property tax records online, get me a list of anyone with D-O-N or D-A-W-N in their name?"

"Unfortunately, no," Esther said.

"But property tax records are a matter of public record anywhere in the U.S.," Gray insisted.

"That doesn't mean they have to be published online," Samuel pointed out. "And NSB does not."

Gray felt his excitement slip away. "But if I want to pursue this avenue of investigation—other Dons—what do you propose?"

Samuel exchanged another glance with Esther, then both of them began laughing. "We've got just the thing," Esther said, reaching into a credenza drawer, then pushing a paperbound volume across the conference table to Gray.

The white pages. The actual, printed phone book white pages. A small volume by any standard, but still a hundred or more pages of small print listings.

It seemed Gray had his work cut out for him.

Samuel had no spare office for Gray. In fact, the only private office in the suite was Samuel's own (a tight little cubby indeed), with Esther typically doing her own work from a small desk in the suite's reception area. As the two of them went about their own tasks, Gray kept his seat at the conference room table, settling in to start searching for other Dons.

But *not* in the phone book she'd just handed him. Just like when someone insisted on giving him directions to their house or favorite restaurant, he smiled and nodded... then sought the information online. In this day and age, Gray refused to believe the Internet wasn't the best source of public information.

This time, however, he was quickly disabused of that notion. Using his phone, he first confirmed what Samuel claimed, that North Slope Borough—unlike the five boroughs of New York City—did *not* publish property tax records online. So next he went to the white pages online... and discovered that website didn't even recognize 'Utqiaġvik' or 'North Slope' as valid locations, returning a 'City not found' error. Nearby 'Atqasuk' *was* recognized, but returned over seven hundred results, which obviously couldn't be right for a population of just two hundred fifty.

Gray glanced up to find Esther watching him through the open conference room door, a knowing smirk on her face. Sighing, he dug a highlighter from the pen cup on the table and reached for the phone book. He found the Utqiaġvik listings and quickly skimmed through a few pages, confirming that Don and variant names really were uncommon here. And yet... With a suspicious frown, he estimated the number of names per page, multiplying that by the number of pages... "There are only a couple thousand listings for Utqiaġvik," he called to her. "That's less than half the population, isn't it?"

"What did you expect?" Esther laughed. "We may be rural, but we're not backward. Almost everyone uses unlisted cell phones now, and most people have gotten rid of their home phones."

Of course. Gray should have known better, but when he'd finally accepted that going through a *phone book* was his best course of action, some part of him—the pretentious, East Coast part—really had assumed this was a place forgotten by time.

"Hey, don't look so glum," Samuel said, emerging from his office. He walked over and dropped a sheet of paper in front of Gray.

"What's this?" the P.I. asked in surprise.

"A list of all NSB citizens with D-O-N or D-A-W-N anywhere in their name, complete with property tax addresses."

"But you said—"

"I said our property taxes weren't online," Samuel interrupted, and now *he* was the one smirking. "I didn't say they weren't computerized. I just had to ask Tammy in the assessor's office. She faxed them right over."

"See?" Esther said innocently. "We're modern here."

"Fax is modern?" Gray muttered.

Samuel boomed a laugh. "Well, I did make my request via email. But Tammy herself is still a little old-fashioned."

"So what was *this* all about?" Gray asked, indicating the phone book. "Having fun at the tunnuq's expense?"

"Maybe a little," Esther said. Both Iñupiat were wearing matching grins, and Gray couldn't help but smile too. He decided he liked these two very much.

"It says a lot about a person, how they take a joke," Samuel put in. "Besides, you *can* use the white pages to cross-reference at least some of Tammy's names, since her data only includes addresses, no phone numbers."

Gray looked over the list of names and addresses as Samuel returned to his cubby. There were just fifteen good matches living in the NSB's eight villages (not counting any oil field employees, who of course weren't full-time residents). Exactly nine lived here in Utqiaġvik: four Donalds as either first or middle name, one Donovan, two Donnas, and one Dawna—plus a single individual with the *surname* Don. Tammy at the assessor's office had also included some flimsier matches—a couple Brandons and Gordons, and even an Adonijah (which *was* a Biblical name, apparently)—but Gray set those aside for now. All told, it would still be a lot of individuals for one investigator to chase down, but far from unmanageable.

When Gray was with the NYPD, this avenue of investigation would have been completely infeasible. Out of 8.5 million souls in New York City's five boroughs, the number of Dons probably outnumbered the entire population of North Slope Borough. It really was a different world above the Arctic Circle, as Gray had observed so many times before.

And yet, it was still part of the larger world, which *wasn't* so large... as Gray saw when they broke for lunch a few hours later. After greeting a delivery driver at the door, Esther laid out a surprising spread on the conference table: chicken panang, shrimp fried rice, and coconut tom kha soup from a Thai place up the street. Gray, Samuel, and Esther shared the food buffet style while getting to know each other on a more personal level, and the surprises kept coming. It turned out Samuel had earned his law degree—in person—from the University of Texas at Austin, and

Esther's favorite hobby was online video gaming. Fantasy RPGs, primarily.

For his part, Gray shared a little about his career as an NYPD homicide detective, but found himself speaking more about his disabilities.

"Tell them to me again?" Samuel asked curiously, reaching for his computer.

"Achromatopsia, hemeralopia, and also prosopagnosia," Gray said with a smile, spelling the strange medical terms out loud as Samuel typed them in. "Color blindness, day blindness, and face blindness."

"No kidding..." the lawyer breathed as he skimmed one article online, then shifted his gaze back to Gray. "So you're saying if we ran into each other on the street tomorrow...?"

"I wouldn't know you from Adam," Gray confirmed. "Of course, if you acted like you knew *me*, I'd start paying more attention. And I've got my own bag of tricks for guessing identities. I'd consider your height, your haircut, your voice—or tattoos, in Esther's case. I've grown to love Iñupiat tattoos for exactly that reason. Context helps too, *where* I encounter a person. And if I still wasn't sure, well, these days I'd probably just admit I'm bad with faces and *ask*."

"These days, you say?" Of course a lawyer would pick up on that. "You weren't always so open about it?"

"No. I hid it for most of the first year after the attack," Gray said, without going into further detail. He relished the freedom of not having to hide any longer—for a while there, all of that lying had turned him into an uglier version of himself—but for the same reason, he didn't like dwelling on that period of his life either.

"I bet that... introduced challenges... for your work as a cop."

Gray just smiled.

"I'm not saying I doubt you," Esther put in between bites of food. "It just seems so unlikely, doesn't it? One person suffering all three of these things?"

Gray shrugged. "Not according to the specialists I've spoken with. They're all related forms of brain damage, apparently. And considering how many blows I took to the head..." He trailed off, noticing their sober expressions. "My dad has fun with it, at least. He likes to strike up random conversations with me in public, say the most outlandish things, and see how long it takes me to figure out who it is I'm talking to. This one time, he pretended to be homeless..."

After lunch, Gray began researching the local Dons, finding out everything he could online, looking for any points of intersection between them and David Simmonds. As part of this, Esther even allowed him to login to her various social media accounts and see what popped up there. Although she and Samuel only knew a handful of these individuals, and none of them well, a small community like Utqiaġvik had only a few degrees of separation between any two locals. Of course, this kind of research only required half of Gray's attention; so while he worked, he and the others discussed various case-related questions as they came to mind, many of them pertaining to David's final video log—which, at present, formed the foundation of the case against Dawn.

"What is this 'awful discovery' David is talking about on the video?" Esther asked after rewatching the early part of the log entry again (but skipping its gruesome end). "And what does he mean, 'it changes everything I thought I knew about what I'm doing'? He was doing whale research, right? Could the murder have something to do with his work?"

It was an excellent question. "We should find out who wrote David's research grant and ask them," Samuel suggested, making a note.

And a few minutes later: "Can we hire someone to enhance the audio?" Gray wanted to know. "See if we can understand what the killer was yelling through the door right before David was killed?"

"We already did, and they couldn't," Esther reported. "Found a film major at UAF who jumped at the chance to help with a murder trial. But it didn't take him long to determine that part of the audio track was just too muffled."

Later, Gray asked, "How confident are we in the validity of the video's timestamp? If there's any question about that, the case against Dawn rather falls apart, doesn't it?"

"I asked the same thing myself," Samuel assured him. "The tech who works for the cloud service said he was willing to testify under oath. The timestamps on all the log files he spot-checked—including that last one—accurately match the metadata, whatever that is. He also assured the police that they couldn't be modified once uploaded."

Gray frowned. "That doesn't make sense. People modify cloud-stored data all the time."

"Apparently these files are version-controlled. If modified on the user's computer, it simply creates a new version in the cloud after upload. Makes it easy to restore data you've accidentally changed or deleted. Very helpful, especially in this case... just not very helpful for Dawn."

"What about Daylight Savings Time?" Esther asked suddenly. It was going to be Gray's next question too. "September was before time change, when we fell back an hour. Does that make a difference?"

Samuel shrugged. "We can't know for sure until we have Dawn's location data and timestamps from that day, but I don't see how. She would've been on DST too."

And Gray wondered aloud what ballistics would show. Based on the devastation caused to David Simmonds' body, it seemed clear he was shot at close range with large caliber FMJ or hard-cast bullets—like the .44 Magnum cartridges police had found loaded in Dawn's Ruger Super Redhawk revolver. But of course, unless and until police found David's boat—and, presumably, the crime scene within it—they would have nothing to compare against to determine if Dawn's gun was the murder weapon.

Something else occurred to Gray sometime in the late afternoon. "If David was killed on the boat, then a bear got to his body, that means his boat must've drifted ashore."

Esther shook her head, confident on this point. "Someone would've spotted it by now. You've seen the landscape around here. It's all flat, empty coastline, and other boats are constantly back and forth through the end of summer."

"Then how did the bear get to the body?" Gray pressed.

"Maybe the killer moved the body?" Samuel theorized. "Then sank the boat so it *wouldn't* ever be found?"

Gray found that possibility unsatisfying. "Move the body for what purpose... unless they *wanted* it to be found? Better to sink the body with the boat, and David Simmonds would simply disappear."

Unfortunately, although Gray knew more now than he had 24 hours ago, he still had more questions than answers.

As the day wound down, he expressed interest in delving further into the video recordings—not just David's last, fatal log entry, but also the longer routine entries that came before. Esther happily transferred the files onto a spare thumb drive, as much history as would fit. When Gray pointed out that he didn't have a computer with him, Samuel drove him to a local electronics store to buy a cheap laptop before dropping him off at his inn for the evening.

On Samuel's recommendation, Gray ordered a pie delivered from one of the nearby pizzerias. He was coming to see that good food was extremely important to Iñupiaq culture, be it traditional fare or dishes borrowed from other ethnicities. Frankly, he should have realized this long ago, considering food was the entire basis of his relationship with Dawn until now. As for the local pizza joints, both boasted New York style pies—and indeed, the one he ordered wasn't half bad. Gray could *hear* the order taker's amusement over the phone, when he requested three types of cheese, four types of meat, and garlic baked into the crust, but the pie that arrived half an hour later included everything he requested. It was simply the dough that couldn't be faked. Authentic New York pizza dough could only be mixed using authentic New York City municipal water, after all.

Settling into a carb coma post-dinner, Gray pulled out his new laptop and plugged in Esther's thumb drive. He watched a few of David Simmonds' log entries, but they were highly detailed and highly scientific, the biologist droning on monotonously about mating and migration patterns in a way that soon had Gray snoozing fitfully.

He woke to the ringing of his phone. It was his father.

"*Grayson*," Old Gray greeted him, his voice laden with mild reproof. "*I've been waiting patiently all day to hear from you.*" That wasn't entirely true. By Gray's count, the elder Gaynes had texted at least three times since yesterday, when Gray had sent his own message about not flying home. Gray had responded, of course—he didn't want his dad to worry—but not in any great detail. "*Is everything okay?*" the old man asked now.

"I'm fine, Dad."

"*Then...*" Old Gray trailed off expectantly.

Gray hesitated only briefly before relenting. "A woman I know was accused of murder," he began. Belatedly, Gray realized he probably should have told his father weeks ago, when the arrest first happened; but at times, their relationship was more like roommates than father-son. "I don't suppose it made the news cycle down there?"

"*I might have heard something. The brother and sister?*"

"That's right." Even in southern Alaska, where most of the population lived, murder was uncommon enough to make the news each time. "Let's just say I'm... skeptical... she had anything to do with the crime. So I'm assisting her lawyer as a private investigator, to make sure she gets a fair hearing."

There was a long, surprised pause. Then: "*Grayson, that's wonderful.*"

Gray blinked. "I'm sorry?"

"*Oh, not that that there was a murder. But* you. *It's wonderful that* you *are using your talents once more, pursuing truth as you once did. I'm so happy for you, son.*"

"I... well, thank you, Dad."

They talked a bit more, Gray explaining a little about Dawn and the case against her. "*Good for you, son, truly,*" Old Gray eventually repeated. "*I guess this means you're going to miss Christmas, though?*"

Gray winced. Yes, Christmas was now just five days away. What's worse, he'd worked the Christmas hitch both of his first two seasons as a roustabout; this would've been their first chance to celebrate together in several years. "I guess so, Dad. Sorry."

"*Just make sure you have everything wrapped up by the time Vera comes to visit, yes?*"

Gray gave a start. With everything going on, he'd barely thought of Vera in weeks—and Vera wasn't the sort of woman you generally forgot.

Sometime last year, Gray had decided he was finally ready to start dating again. The only problem: dating in Alaska was more challenging than elsewhere, thanks to a variety of factors. For one thing, the pool of eligible singles was small, and many—like Gray—worked seasonal schedules. Then there was the skewed gender ratio, the fact that men outnumbered women here. When Gray had casually told his neighbor he might give dating another go, the man had scoffed: "Get in line and wait your turn."

Instead, Gray had cautiously reached out to Vera Vecoli, a woman he'd dated a few times in NYC before realizing he wasn't ready. To his surprise, she was still single too. Sure, she'd been in multiple relationships during the seven years since, a few serious, but none had worked out in the end. So they'd begun talking every couple weeks by phone.

Of course, getting serious about a relationship with Vera presented its own challenge: she was there, and he was here. But eventually, she broached the subject of coming to visit him—not on the North Slope, of course, but down in Anchorage where Gray and Old Gray shared a house between hitches. Who knew? Maybe she would fall in love with Alaska. It was a story he'd heard more than a few times from adopted locals, of coming to visit a friend for a week and never leaving. Not that it seemed likely with a highly successful ad executive like Vera Vecoli, but... well, stranger things had happened. Just look at some of the weird cases he'd investigated.

Regardless, the day of her arrival in Alaska was fast approaching, now just—he checked his phone calendar—four weeks away. The prospect of that visit filled Gray's heart with excitement and dread in equal measure. And suddenly, he felt guilty too.

While he didn't usually speak with Vera while in U-Turn, he *did* usually call after returning to Anchorage—meaning she would have expected a call yesterday or today. Plus, he really should tell her about the case. She would probably be as excited and supportive as Old Gray.

"I'd better go, Dad. I owe Vera a call too."

"*I'm proud of you, son. Give that lovely young lady my regards, and tell her I look forward to finally meeting her in person next month.*"

"I will. Love you, Dad."

It was only after hanging up with his father that Gray remembered the time difference. It was almost 8 p.m. here in Alaska, which made it close to midnight on the East Coast—and Vera was the early-to-bed, early-to-rise type. With a sigh, he jotted off a quick email instead, then collapsed into bed early himself.

The rest of that week

Utqiaġvik

The next morning, Gray started chasing down Utqiaġvik's nine Dons.

He called the NSBPD detectives first, as a courtesy, having gotten their cell numbers from Samuel. Committed to transparency with local law enforcement, Gray said he was looking into other individuals with similar names to Dawn and was happy to share his findings—unless the detectives were planning to explore that avenue of investigation themselves? Jameson told Gray to knock himself out, and sure, to pass along anything he learned. The tunnuq cop was polite enough about it, but he clearly didn't expect Gray to find anything.

Samuel picked him up from his inn, then Gray dropped the lawyer at his office and borrowed his pickup truck for the day. His first stop after that was a local copy shop, to take possession of the full box of business cards he had ordered yesterday. This new version was still simple, black text on white cardstock, now including phone number and email address... but printed this time with raised text. It was amazing the legitimacy that raised text granted, even if it cost a mere $10 more. So armed, Gray finally started knocking on doors.

It proved a much easier proposition than expected. On the congested streets of New York City, it might've taken Gray days, even a week, to visit so many persons of interest—longer depending how many were away from home when he dropped by. Not so in this quiet, 20-square-mile village of 5,000. Crisscrossing the town's simple street grid in Samuel's truck, Gray managed to find and interview six of the nine likeliest names that very first day. Not all were at home, of course, but usually a family member or neighbor directed Gray to a nearby place of business.

In his experience, most guilty people weren't very good at pretending the right kind of surprise when an investigator showed up asking unexpected questions. After introducing himself to the Dons on his list, proffering his new card, Gray would hit them with the relevant questions before they had a chance to find equilibrium: "Are you Donald Hopson? Donovan Bodfish? Donna Tukle? Are you familiar with David Simmonds? Did you have any reason to want him dead?"

Most of the men and women were indeed familiar with the victim—maybe not by name, but certainly once Gray explained that David was the big-time marine biologist who drove that monstrous yacht back and forth along the coast every year, all summer long. Some of the Dons got angry at the very mention of the man, freely admitting he was an embarrassment to their people. Others expressed regret over past ill will, now that he'd turned up dead. Everyone already knew of his demise, of course, for that news had easily spread throughout their tight-knit community over the last two weeks. And *everyone* was surprised to find a P.I. at the door asking questions. What mattered was, no one Gray interviewed that first day showed the kind of surprise that raised his suspicions.

Unfortunately, something like the 80-20 rule proved true when he tried to finish up the last three strong matches the next day. Two proved as easy as the ones the day before, but Gray kept just-missing a 24-year-old man named Aaron Don throughout the day—first at the apartment he shared with his grandmother, then twice at the auto repair shop where he worked. The first time Gray dropped by, Aaron was supposedly on break, and the second time he had just gone home sick. When Gray swung by the man's rental unit again that night, the grandmother claimed she hadn't seen him. Gray wasn't fooled. He knew by now that the young man was dodging him.

So, come 5 a.m. the *next* morning, Gray and Esther were parked up the street in her SUV—almost everyone here drove trucks or SUVs—waiting for the appearance of the young man Gray increasingly suspected of *something*. Of course, being a Saturday, the boy had probably decided to sleep late. It wasn't until well after 11 that Esther sat up straight and pointed at a slight figure emerging from the apartment building, then getting into a parked car. "That's him!" This was, of course, why she had joined Gray on the stakeout, precisely because he wasn't capable of making identification on his own.

Putting the SUV in gear, they pulled forward and stopped in such a way as to block Aaron from pulling out. Rounding the other vehicle, Gray pressed his business card against the driver's side window and yelled, since the driver refused to lower the glass even a crack. "Aaron Don? I'm Grayson Gaynes, private investigator. Are you familiar with—"

Gray didn't get a chance to ask about David Simmonds, for the suspect chose that moment to throw his door open and make a run for it—definitely the wrong kind of surprise! Aaron obviously intended to knock Gray over, though Gray anticipated the move and sidestepped. Still on his feet, the former cop probably could have chased the boy down easily, tackling and cuffing him in short order, but... well, he *wasn't* a cop anymore, and had no authority to make arrests (much less any handcuffs). Instead, he quickly phoned Detective Jameson and made him aware of Aaron Don's suspicious behavior.

It wasn't until late that evening that police finally cornered and interviewed the young man, eventually teasing out the truth: Aaron Don had been stealing cash from the register at work for months now, whenever necessary to make rent, and he'd panicked when a P.I. started poking around. He *was* guilty, just not of murdering David Simmonds, whom he'd never even heard of. Jameson laughed out loud at the confession, clasping a crestfallen Gray on one shoulder and wishing him a Merry Christmas before going home to his own family.

All told, ruling out Aaron Don had taken more of Gray's time than his other eight strong Utqiaġvik matches combined. And only then, at 7 p.m. on Saturday night, did he realize his mistake. Tomorrow was Sunday *and* Christmas Eve. There would be no flights out to Nuiqsut—where he'd been planning to go next—until Tuesday, the day after Christmas. Gray's new bush pilot friend Jacob confirmed as much when he called to check. And *driving* certainly wasn't an option, even if Samuel or Esther were willing to loan him a vehicle for the next several days. Community winter access trails did exist between villages, snow roads that were painstakingly recreated each year, but civilians only traveled those routes in escorted caravans—and there wouldn't be another one of those until after Christmas either.

So Gray spent Sunday chasing down as many of Utqiaġvik's less likely Dons as he could: the Brandons, Gordons, and (ahem) Adonijah. And he identified just as many genuine suspects for David's murder as he had in previous days, which was to say none. At least none of these folks wasted as much of his time as Aaron Don.

That night—Christmas Eve—Gray enjoyed a lovely sit-down dinner at his inn with the handful of other guests, then they and the staff sang Christmas carols around the piano until late. And, for the most part, Gray was able to put the case out of his mind and simply enjoy himself. After he returned to his room for the evening, he even got a call from Vera that lasted two hours and left him feeling excited about their relationship.

But as he hung up and started getting ready for bed, Gray felt Dawn's case begin pressing down on him again. Despite all the possible suspects he had ruled out these last four days, he couldn't help but feel like he was spinning his wheels, accomplishing nothing that would actually help get Dawn out of lockup. And then, when he thought of Dawn behind bars on this celebratory night, he felt even worse.

Now thoroughly demoralized, Gray tried and failed to find sleep in this cheerless hotel room at the so-called Top of the World.

Monday, December 25th

Utqiaġvik

On Christmas morning, Gray startled awake to the sound of his phone ringing again. Of course, it was still pitch black outside, so he had to check the phone's display to see it was already after 9 a.m. He had not slept well.

"Hello?" he managed.

"*Get up and get dressed,*" Samuel ordered. "*I'll be there in half an hour to get you.*"

Gray sat up straight. "What is it? Break in the case?"

Samuel laughed over the line. "*Of course not. Today is Christmas, and my wife reminded me no one should spend Christmas in a hotel room.*"

"Oh," Gray said, sagging back into his bed. "That's okay, but thank you."

"Nonsense. Did Santa Claus deliver any gifts to you there last night?"

Gray glanced around the little room. "No."

"I didn't think so, because they're all here. Got your name on 'em and everything. So I'll see you in half an hour." And he hung up before Gray could object further.

Gray realized he was grinning. So he got up and got ready to spend Christmas with the Leavitts.

Samuel's wife Meredith was the last thing Gray expected: an athletic blonde almost as tall as Samuel, her long hair in matted braids, her face split by a permanent smile even bigger than her husband's. It seemed they and their children, 11-year-old Aurora and 9-year-old Luca, had been waiting on Gray to arrive before attacking their large brunch of smoked arctic char, boiled potatoes, fry bread, and caviar of all things. Then they went straight to opening gifts, Gray included. Samuel wasn't kidding. There were a half dozen beautifully wrapped presents under the tree for him, and if most of them were obviously regifts, he didn't mind. A man could never have enough summer sausages, chocolate samplers, gourmet whole-bean coffee, or thick woolen socks.

A lot of the Leavitt family's Christmas traditions felt familiar to Gray, while others were beyond strange, and he quickly gave up trying to figure out which were actually Iñupiat. Meredith herself was Texan, having fallen in love with Samuel when he attended law school in her home state. The two of them freely admitted to reappropriating any fun tradition, no matter where it came from—then asked what traditions *Gray*'s family practiced on

Christmas Day. Surprised, he stammered out that he and his dad often enjoyed a rousing game of chess.

Within moments, their daughter Aurora was setting up the pieces. Gray took it easy on her the first round, and she quickly trounced him. So on the rematch, he paid more attention while chatting with Samuel about the case.

"I've made zero progress figuring out who wrote David's research grant," the lawyer admitted. "It definitely wasn't federally funded, or the information would already be public."

"Did you check with the university?" Gray asked, wincing as Aurora took one of his knights—which had *not* been part of his meager strategy. "Where'd David get his PhD again?"

"UAF." That was University of Alaska at Fairbanks, Gray knew. "And yes," Samuel confirmed, "I checked with them. Spoke at length with the dean of the College of Fisheries and Ocean Sciences, then sent emails to every other faculty member in that department."

"Email? Not phone?" Gray moved a pawn.

"Oh, now you're concerned my methods are *too* modern?" Samuel quipped. "Yeah, they're all on winter break, so no one was answering their office phones. Plus, it's easy to mail-merge an entire list of email recipients so each one thinks I'm emailing them individually."

"Okay, okay, you've convinced me," Gray conceded. "Your methods are more modern even than mine."

Samuel accepted the praise magnanimously, then laughed out loud when Aurora took Gray's other knight. "Anyway, I've heard back from a lot of the faculty, some by email, a few by phone. Many of them remember David Simmonds, and with a lot more fondness than folks up here, but none admit to corresponding with him in recent years. And none knew anything about a research grant."

Gray frowned, moving a pawn and asking, "Doesn't that strike you as odd? He must've gotten the grant coming out of their program. *No one* remembers anything about it?"

"Nope."

"And for that matter, wouldn't the community of marine biologists be small enough in this area that people are at least aware of their colleagues' work? Surely *someone* knows what David was researching."

"No one I spoke with," Samuel said heavily. "However, the dean said he would find some volunteers to review David's research logs—after I get NSBPD to approve sharing them—and let me know if anything stands out as unusual or, um, salacious."

It was Gray's turn to laugh. Nothing about biology struck him as particularly salacious. Well, not marine biology anyway.

Aurora checkmated Gray a second time, but he managed to end their third match in a stalemate. Then it was 9-year-old Luca's turn to get Gray's attention, something he'd been patiently awaiting. He wanted Gray to quiz him, on anything and everything, from U.S. presidents to states of the union to World War II history. When they exhausted those topics (more quickly than Gray was proud of), Luca was eager to teach *Gray* a few things about Iñupiaq culture.

"We use a base-20 counting system," the fourth grader told him proudly.

Gray blinked. "I don't know what that means."

"Most people use base-10," Luca explained. "You call it decimal. Ten different numerals—you know, zero through nine?"

"Okay, sure, I follow you now." Gray's eyes widened a little. "And you're saying the Iñupiat have *twenty* different numerals?" The boy nodded proudly. "Write them for me," Gray demanded.

And the boy did: 𝋀, 𝋁, 𝋂, 𝋃, 𝋄, 𝋅, 𝋆, 𝋇, 𝋈, 𝋉, 𝋊, 𝋋, 𝋌, 𝋍, 𝋎, 𝋏, 𝋐, 𝋑, 𝋒, and 𝋓. "Zero to nineteen," he announced proudly. "And twenty is the first number requiring two digits," he concluded, adding it at the bottom: 𝋁𝋀.

The symbols were completely foreign to Gray. Should he be embarrassed by that, after two seasons on the slope? There really wasn't *that* much chance to experience local culture in a tunnuq work camp, conversations with Dawn notwithstanding. "Wait, there's a pattern to these numbers," Gray realized.

“You’ve got a good eye!” the 9-year-old praised the former cop seriously, drawing a smile from everyone. “Even if you haven’t memorized all these numerals, you can still figure them out by counting the slashes. Every up-down slash counts as *one*, and every left-right slash counts as *five*.” He began pointing to the figures he had written down. “So this V-like character is the number *two*, and this W-like character is *four*. But if it has one cross slash at the top, like here”——“that’s five plus four, or *nine.*”

Aurora shouldered her way into the conversation. “And this one with *two* horizontal slashes is fourteen”——“while this one with *three* horizontals is nineteen”—.

“Hey!” Luca complained. “You already had your turn.”

“Remarkable,” Gray said. “Not just these numbers, but the two of you.” Both children beamed at that. “I wish you could meet my friend Bobbi. Knowing her, she would get a kick out of talking number systems and culture and probably cryptography with you two.”

“Ooh!” Luca squealed. “I *love* cryptography!”

“Of course you do,” Gray laughed.

In the afternoon, the entire family plus Gray went to visit Dawn at the community jail. The fact that Samuel would bring his children to meet his client, an accused murderer, was a remarkable show of faith—especially considering the doubts he had previously expressed to Gray. And the gesture obviously touched Dawn deeply.

Gray knew her instantly when she entered the supervised visitation hall. She was hardly the only incarcerated person receiving a visit, today of all days, so Gray shouldn't have been so certain of her identity. Yet he felt he would recognize that face anywhere. Her tattoos were part of it—the V on her forehead, the distinctive arcs on her cheeks, the five stripes on her chin—but Gray imagined a sparkling kindness to those features that was unique to her. Somehow, Dawn Simmonds radiated joy despite her circumstances, despite even her fear of the future.

She took great delight in meeting the children, her cheeks moist as she thanked Samuel and Meredith again and again for bringing them along. She said little to Gray, but her warm gaze returned to him often enough that he felt her blazing gratitude as well.

Today being Christmas and this a small facility in a small community, the typical restrictions against food and physical touch were relaxed, though the guard presence was doubled during visiting hours. Meredith had brought a peppermint Texas sheet cake with lots of paper plates and plastic utensils, enough for other families to share. Everyone, even the corrections officers, laughed when Dawn asked if there was any contraband baked into the cake. She then had to explain the jail bake trope to Luca, who had no idea people used to smuggle skeleton keys and iron files to prisoners inside baked goods.

With the kids present, they didn't talk a lot about the case; but that was probably as it should be, Gray decided. Christmas was a day to focus on the positive, not the negative. If Dawn herself hadn't asked for an update, it wouldn't have come up at all.

"Right now, we're looking into alternate suspects," Gray said.

"It wasn't me," she told Gray emphatically, eyes wide and intense, begging him to believe her.

Gray peered deeply into those windows to her soul. "I believe you," he assured her, even as his inner skeptic continued to doubt his own instincts. "Have *you* thought of anyone else with motive?" he asked hopefully.

"Real motive, no," she sighed. "Just lots of people who didn't like him."

"Anyone else named Don—male or female—or Donny or Donetta or anything like that?"

But Dawn was already shaking her head. "It's just not a common name around here."

Gray nodded, not surprised, but glad he'd asked. Just to be sure.

"What was your brother studying?" Samuel spoke up.

"Whale migration patterns," she said, same as she'd told Gray the last time he saw her, in U-Turn's NSBPD substation two weeks prior.

"And who funded his research grant?" the lawyer pressed.

"I don't know. Some private institute. That's all he ever told me. Not... not that I showed much interest or supported him." Dawn seemed to shrink back into herself. "He was my little brother, and I scoffed at what he was doing with his life. I was just so *angry* over the way he was behaving!"

Gray gave her a sad smile, but didn't try to minimize her grief. "I'm sorry," he said simply.

Dawn seemed to rally. "But I *am* innocent. And I won't stop fighting these charges, if only because I want to make sure his real killer is found." She caught Luca staring at her with round eyes. "Um, sorry, Samuel."

Samuel waved it off. "And you can't tell us anything else about this private institute?"

She shook her head. "I just know they were loaded. Rich, I mean. Paid for David's yacht and all the retrofitting for his equipment. That alone had to cost millions, not counting ongoing expenses. And still David seemed to be drowning in money. It was the way he flashed his wealth around that disgusted everyone," she reminded them.

By then, Meredith was giving Samuel a look, so everyone steered the conversation toward safer topics. Within minutes, Dawn was quizzing Luca on his Iñupiaq vocabulary—something he didn't actually get to use on a day-to-day basis.

"Stay strong," Gray told Dawn later, as they stood to leave. "We're fighting for you. It may not happen fast, but we'll get to the truth." How he wished for that to be true.

"I believe you," she assured him, repeating his own words from earlier. Then she surprised Gray by throwing her arms around him and squeezing tight. "Thank you," she whispered, breath warm in his ear.

The nearest guard gave a quiet cough, causing Dawn to step back hurriedly. And with that, their visit ended, the Iñupiaq woman escorted back into the bowels of the facility. Between the cake and that fierce hug, Dawn would probably be frisked quite thoroughly before returning to her cell, but Gray appreciated the extra grace the corrections officers were extending today.

"What?" he asked Meredith when he caught her watching him intently.

Her face broke into a slow smile. "Oh, nothing."

Tuesday, December 26th
Nuiqsut

First thing the next morning, Gray was winging his way back to Nuiqsut in Jacob's Cessna 185. Samuel concurred that the Simmonds' hometown was the best place to continue Gray's investigation, interviewing not only alternate Dons but also those who'd known David and Dawn in their youth. Plus, Nuiqsut was where David's body had been discovered... so to speak.

Of course, flying direct to Nuiqsut out of Utqiaġvik was a deviation from Jacob's normal postal service route; but by now, the bush pilot knew about Gray's connection to the David Simmonds case and happily rearranged his flight schedule to accommodate the private investigator. It wasn't that Jacob had any stake in proving Dawn's innocence, just that a murder trial was a serious thing. Regardless of which side Gray was working for—prosecution or defense—Jacob insisted he would do his part to help prevent delays in the investigation.

Gray believed the man, mostly. He also recognized that Jacob was a man bursting with curiosity under pretty much any circumstances. And sure enough, the pilot was just as full of questions as last time, now wanting to know how an oil company roughneck was qualified to be a P.I. on a big murder case. Appreciative of the lift to Nuiqsut, Gray obligingly gave him a thumbnail sketch of his past. In turn, Gray asked after Jacob's Christmas with his wife and four kids, and the pilot smiled delightedly that Gray remembered hearing about them.

Before long, Jacob was happily gabbing about Iñupiat post-Christmas festivities, like the 'married vs. single' games that were played from December 26th through 30th each year. And when they landed at Nuiqsut a short time later, Gray was engaged enough that he only half noticed their shuddering touchdown on the gravel airstrip.

Alas, Nuiqsut soon proved a bust on the alternate-Don-murderer front. Out of a population of 500, there were only a Donald and a Donatella, both of whom he quickly ruled out (the former in his eighties, the latter wheelchair bound). By lunchtime, Gray was reviewing his list of less-likely matches (namely, a local Landon), when he saw the entire village begin moving toward the community center. It was time for the annual married vs. single games.

So, with nothing else to do, he joined them.

There was some initial surprise at his appearance—but again, not the wrong kind of surprise. In a community this small, everyone knew everyone, and visitors were especially uncommon in winter. But Gray sought out the village elder he'd spoken with last night by phone, one of the ones Dawn had been working with to plan David's funeral, before her arrest. The older man immediately took Gray under his wing and began introducing him around. And when the locals saw Gray address the man respectfully as 'aapaaluk' or even 'aapa' for short—grandfather—they warmed to him quickly.

Gray was not prepared for the games, despite Jacob's stories. Of course, he never dreamed he'd be invited to participate. But he *was* single, so he soon had a loop of string around one ear, connecting him to a loop around a local husband's ear. Thus did they face off, pulling away from each other and grimacing in pain while the crowd cheered them on; and Gray did not submit until the string broke, earning him more goodwill. Immediately thereafter, however, he proved himself inept at filleting and cleaning a raw fish, and he didn't even try to make a pot of tea on the camp stove. Grinning despite himself, Gray began to see the rationale behind these activities. Like the more famous Northern Games, these were tests of the sorts of survival skills Iñupiat traditionally needed in this harsh environment. Even the ear pull gauged a man's ability to endure pain. As for pitting the marrieds against the singles, that was just for fun, a way of fostering community during the holidays.

And between games, Gray ate. Oh, how he ate, for the spread of food was magnificent. He tried moose and caribou (flown up special from Nome), along with locally produced maktak (whale skin and blubber), tuktak (fermented walrus flipper), and goose soup with unsweetened fried doughnuts. And for dessert, he gorged himself on akutaq 'ice cream' with wild berries.

For a time, he even forgot he was there in a professional capacity, and that was probably a good thing. He mingled, got to know a number of people personally, smiled and joked. When the David Simmonds murder eventually came up, it did so organically, the locals asking Gray for updates or curious about his involvement. As a result, his own questions then felt less invasive.

Gray confirmed that Dawn and David's parents were indeed deceased. That had happened a long time ago, first him and then her, nothing suspicious. Both had been older than usual when they met and married, Dawn's mother a free-spirited child of the sixties who eventually found her way here from the lower 48. It was through Dawn's father that she derived her Native Alaskan heritage—which wasn't unusual, as Gray had already learned from Samuel. Though it sounded crass to hear the locals say it in so many words, there were few full-blooded Iñupiat anymore. Intermarriage with tunnuq, or 'mixed blood', was the norm here. Perhaps even more so than the rest of the world, Gray was starting to realize.

With David gone, Dawn had no other surviving relatives, though of course the entire village was family. No one here truly believed she had murdered her own brother—the two had been so close as children!—and honestly, the Nuiqsut community had never felt much animosity to David. Of course, being inland, they hadn't seen as much of him or his monster boat as their friends and family up in coastal Utqiaġvik. As for David's current studies or the identity of his increasingly mysterious sponsor, the villagers had zero insight. Gray met both of Nuiqsut's NSBPD officers, and one even complimented him on his ear pull technique, though neither would discuss the case. The friendlier cop *did* introduce Gray to the man who shot the problem bear, emptying all five Casull .454 rounds from his Smith & Wesson 460V into the beast's chest and face when it charged his daughter. That had been the first time anyone saw the aggressive animal, confirming popular opinion that it had only just moved into the area from elsewhere. Gray even spoke with—and ruled out—the last of Nuiqsut's Dons, a 20-year-old college student (named Landon) who'd been at school in Anchorage on the day of the murder.

And Gray got to know Jeannette, who claimed to be Dawn's best and oldest friend. Amid story after story of the girls' antics as teenagers, Gray obediently entered the woman's name and number into his phone, promising repeatedly that he *would* call her if there was ever *anything* she could do to help Dawn in her current troubles.

In general, Gray was encouraged by the show of support for Dawn, and he secured promises from several individuals to act as character witnesses if needed. It didn't surprise him to learn that Dawn had been a bright light in this community as well. To hear them tell it, the worst thing she'd ever done was leave each winter to set up shop in that tunnuq work camp sixty miles west of here (though they said this with a grin or wink, so Gray understood they were joking). Yes, Dawn was one of their favorite daughters. No way she had killed David or anyone else.

Gray only worried this confidence would waver once they began to hear some of the evidence against her. And unfortunately, a rather staggering weight of new evidence presented itself that very evening.

Samuel's phone call came at half past 8 p.m., as the day's festivities were winding down. It seemed that, unbeknownst to him, the cloud storage service had finally responded to the warrant on Dawn's phone sometime Saturday—but with the holidays, police had not acted on the new information until today. The deleted texts had been provided, complete with the coordinates David had proposed for the September 13 rendezvous with his sister. "*I'm sending you a screenshot*," the lawyer told Gray. "*Let me know when you've got it.*"

"I've got it," Gray said absently, already scanning the texts David and Dawn had traded the afternoon before David's murder. "What's that first word?" he asked. "Is that a name he's calling her?"

"*Nayaaluk? Means little sister.*"

Gray nodded, still reading. The exchange was displayed from the perspective of Dawn's account:

DAVID ▶

Tues, Sept 12 at 3:58 PM

Nayaaluk, I want to clear the air. Apologize in preson for everything. Before I sail south for the witner. Meet me tomorrow?

Hello?

Dawn?

Fine. Where?

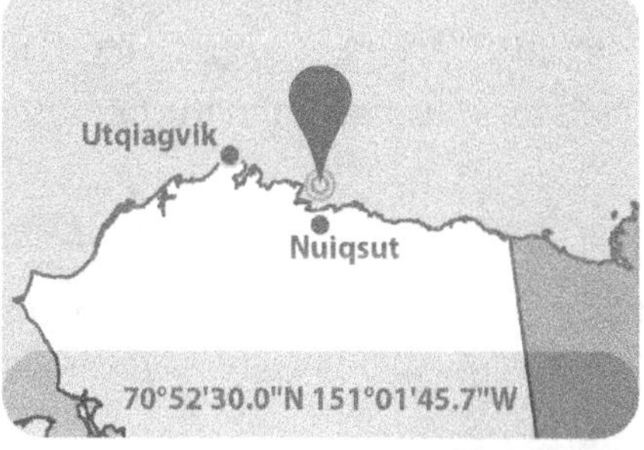

Seriously? Not Utq?

Easier to just meet here I can finally show you the Bowhead

Please Dawn?

What time

1130am plaese dont be late. Something I want to show you.

That was it, the last text messages to be shared between brother and sister.

Samuel went on to say that NSBPD officers out of Utqiaġvik had investigated the coordinates before the lawyer even learned about them. Early today, at the same time Gray was in transit to Nuiqsut, detectives had been hitching a ride on a Search & Rescue chopper to scope out that meeting location—itself due north of Nuiqsut, roughly thirty miles offshore. And sure enough, they had found the *Bowhead II*. Exactly where Dawn claimed she had waited for an hour before giving up to return home.

"What, really?" Gray asked incredulously. "Three and a half months later, and the boat is still just floating there?"

"*Oh, it doesn't have much of a choice,*" Samuel responded drily over the line. "*The yacht is stuck fast. You know in winter, the ocean surface freezes solid as much as fifty miles offshore?*"

Gray *had* heard that, actually. He just wasn't sure he'd ever believed it.

"*It would've happened within a few weeks of those texts,*" Samuel went on. "*So yes, assuming the boat was anchored there on September 13, it's entirely plausible it would've stayed put long enough for the ice to encroach and seal it in. And of course, once it was accessible across the ice, it was only a matter of time before the bears found it.*" With a dark chuckle, the Iñupiaq lawyer dropped another fun nugget of trivia. "*Bears can smell a whale kill from over a hundred miles away, and they're opportunistic. They'll eat just about anything.*"

"So what did the cops find on the boat?" Gray was eager to know.

Samuel hesitated, his tone sober again when he continued. "*More of David, for one thing. Dismembered and strewn across one of the cabins—obviously the same cabin from the video. Blood and gore spatter across the back wall. And all three slugs fired from the murderer's weapon were still embedded in the bulkhead. The NSB cops cut them free and submitted them to the state police lab for ballistics testing.*"

This kind of procedure was quite familiar to a former detective like Gray, of course. "Do they anticipate any trouble getting conclusive results?"

"*No,*" Samuel said confidently. "*These're hard-cast solid bullets, all retrieved in good condition, and of course there's three of them. With Dawn's revolver to discharge and compare against, the lab should have no trouble determining if hers was the murder weapon.*" He hesitated again. "*But that's not all they found, unfortunately.*"

Gray could tell he wasn't going to like this.

"*Crime scene techs went over the cabin inch by inch and collected lots of samples, including fibers and hair strands that they'll submit for DNA. They also lifted several very clear fingerprints... which they've already matched to Dawn.*"

Gray squeezed his eyes shut. "They found her prints on a boat she swears she never boarded."

"*Yes.*"

"And that boat was exactly where her brother told her to meet him. In a text she apparently deleted."

Audible sigh. "*Yes.*"

Gray groaned. "I'd like to see the crime scene for myself, if possible. I assume they towed the boat back to harbor?"

"*Well, no. It's stuck in the ice, remember? They won't be towing it anywhere until the spring thaw. So unless you can convince Search & Rescue to fly you back out there—and the NSBPD to let them—you're out of luck.*"

Gray thought for a moment. "I could just drive, right? You say it's frozen over?"

Samuel barked a laugh. "*You'd have to be a special kind of touched to attempt that. It's possible, sure, but the ice is hardly stable. Ocean currents are still pretty strong beneath the surface, enough to break it up into floes without warning.* I *certainly wouldn't drive out there. Not unless you've got a death wish.*"

"I can't just do nothing, Samuel."

"*Fortunately for you, you won't have to. I have something else I want you to look into, if you're willing.*"

"What's that?"

"*Assuming Dawn really is telling the truth, that means she must've made a mistake—shown up at the rendezvous at the wrong time, or else at the wrong location entirely.*"

"Her phone's location history should show that, one way or the other. It was in the data the cloud folks shared, right?"

"*Nope. Because she had location services turned off too, just like her brother.*"

"Gah!" Gray expressed his frustration, then realized it was worse than that—an accused murderer not only deleting incriminating texts but *also*, apparently, masking her location the day of the murder? As with so much else about this case, it looked bad. "Wait," Gray said, something occurring to him. "She drove her boat out to the middle of the ocean."

"*That's actually the Beaufort Sea, but yes.*"

"Whatever, the sea. My point is, no landmarks. So... how would she know where to go without GPS service?"

Samuel was obviously smiling when he responded. "*Exactly. Which is why I gave Dawn a ring via ICS tonight.*" Gray knew that was an inmate phone service a lot of jails were now using. "*She says her cabin cruiser is equipped with Starlink. It's a satellite positioning system. Lots of locals have them on their boats.*"

Gray felt a glimmer of hope. "So..."

"So I want you to get back to Dawn's place and check the trip history on her Starlink. She says she keeps the boat parked in back in the winter."

"She does," Gray confirmed. "I've seen it." He shook his head, annoyed at himself. "Why didn't anyone think of this before now? You, me, Dawn, *or* the cops? We could've gotten those coordinates without waiting on the warrant."

"We're all just human here, even you. Besides, don't murder investigations usually take a while? I think we're moving along at a pretty steady pace."

Samuel wasn't wrong. Though Gray had certainly closed a few cases rapidly in his former career, complex murder investigations often required months or years. Still, he felt an unusual degree of pressure in this instance. Not only did he want to get Dawn out of lockup; he was also keenly aware of Vera's upcoming visit, less than a month away. For that matter, he was expected back at work with his crew just one week from today, and daily twelve-hour shifts hardly left room for much investigation.

"I'd just as soon keep up that steady pace," Gray told the lawyer, his tone all business. "Back to Dawn's place it is. I'll make sure I'm on the next flight to U-Turn."

Wednesday, December 27th

U-Turn

Except there was no direct flight back to U-Turn from Nuiqsut, unless Gray convinced Jacob to disrupt his schedule again... and the bush pilot wasn't even planning a stop in Nuiqsut tomorrow, having already delivered several days of accumulated mail this morning. The low volume of correspondence in and out of the smaller villages simply didn't justify daily service.

So Gray took Jeannette up on her offer, informing Dawn's oldest friend that it would greatly help Dawn if Gray could borrow her snowmobile for the sixty-mile trek to U-Turn.

To his surprise, Jeannette refused.

Apologetically, she explained that she couldn't afford to lose the use of her 'snow machine' until he returned, especially since he couldn't tell her how long that would be. But she *would* gladly drive him instead.

Gray didn't appreciate just what a sacrifice that was until they were well underway—and he realized that a snowmobile on open terrain wasn't capable of much better speed than the buses the oil company work crews took on the snow roads each day. Even going just fifty or sixty miles (depending on the exact route taken across the tundra in the dark) could require three hours... and, of course, Jeannette would have to immediately turn around and repeat the journey in reverse to get home in time for work in the morning.

The trip was uneventful, if long and boring. There was no talking over the howling of the wind, and Gray stayed huddled against the woman's back the first half of the trip anyway—fully attired in the same gear he normally wore on the TrephOil drill floor. It was actually a warm night, only -5° F with minimal wind... but semi-exposed on the back of a snowmobile going 20 mph, Gray knew effective windchill was below -30° F. By this point in his new career, he did such rule of thumb calculations easily in his head.

The second half of the trip, Jeannette let Gray drive, making sure the tunnuq was comfortable navigating the tundra if the need ever arose again. The Iñupiaq woman kept her own GPS device zip-tied to the handlebars (which offered integrated hand warmers!), so Gray had no trouble remaining oriented, but she warned him to keep his attention on the terrain—which was often uneven, or hid frozen waterways. The Iñupiat might travel this arctic landscape as a matter of routine, but even the smallest accident could have serious repercussions. If you found yourself stranded in the wilderness with an inoperable snow machine in these conditions, that was essentially a death sentence.

When at last they arrived in U-Turn, it was well after midnight. Gray towed Jeannette into one of the TrephOil cafeterias to refill her thermos with hot coffee. "I can't thank you enough," Gray told her. "Seriously. Dawn has a good friend in you."

She shrugged. "Sounds to me like she's got a good friend in you too."

Back outside again, Gray unstrapped his big duffle from the luggage rack, laughing to think of the miles it had now traveled with him—from U-Turn to Utqiaġvik to Nuiqsut and now back to U-Turn—all in the last week. With one more check to ensure Jeannette had fuel for the return trip, he sent her on her way.

Only then did Gray realize he had another problem: accommodations. The dorms he usually stayed in were only available to on-hitch workers, the specific assignments changing from month to month. There would be no room made up for *him* until next Tuesday, when he was due back on the job. So Gray turned from the brightly-lit company modulars and trudged toward U-Turn's outskirts, where Dawn's part-time helper Ephron lived in his own double-wide trailer. Gray would have needed to visit him in the morning anyway, to borrow the keys to Dawn's place.

He rapped at Ephron's door for several minutes before the stoic Iñupiaq appeared, dark eyes bleary.

Ephron listened patiently as Gray explained, then waved him inside and pointed him to an old couch. He never said a word before returning to his own bedroom.

Dark and early the next morning, Gray phoned Abraham Kanayurak, the sole NSBPD officer stationed in U-Turn. "Hey, Abe, this is Gray Gaynes. I'm officially part of Dawn's defense team now."

"*I heard*," the other man said simply.

"I'm calling to inform you that I'm headed to Dawn's place here shortly. We realized she has a Starlink GPS on her boat. I'd like to check its location history for the day of the murder." Gray paused. "Want to join me there, take the device into evidence at the same time?"

"*Okay. Come on by, then.*"

"Come by your substation, you mean?"

"*No, Dawn's place. I'm already here.*" And with that, Abe hung up.

Gray didn't like the sound of that, so he hurried right over.

The colorless (but yellow) clapboard building appeared no different than usual as Gray approached, the washed-out (but fiery red) sunrise on its side gloriously out of place in this dingy work camp. Tromping up the ramp, Gray almost forgot to scrape his shoes and don booties before entering.

"I'm back here!" a voice called as Gray slammed the door firmly shut behind him.

Inside, Dawn's place was downright depressing, for the first time since Gray discovered it two seasons back. Only one naked bulb was lit in the public dining area, the light strands and jukebox both unplugged. Worse, there was already an air of abandonment about the establishment, a thin layer of dust on that beautiful wooden bar after just two weeks of disuse. Gray hurried behind the bar, pushed through the kitchen, and found a uniformed police officer crouched in Dawn's private living area.

"Abe?"

"Who else?" the cop replied distractedly. He was closely examining the rubber sole of a sturdy work boot, looking back and forth between the boot and his cell phone screen. A dozen other pairs of shoes were strewn about, having apparently been uncovered in a fresh search of the house today.

"What's that?" Gray asked, his sense of unease deepening.

Abe glanced at him. Then, without a word, he angled the phone so Gray could see what it displayed: a photograph of a bloody boot print... one with the exact same tread pattern as the boot in Abe's latex-gloved hand. "From the scene of the crime," he noted.

Gray swore inwardly. "Hardly conclusive," he forced himself to say. "These boots could have been planted here by the real murderer. And even if they are really Dawn's, I'm sure plenty of other people have the exact same pair of shoes."

"There's such a thing as a preponderance of evidence," Abe said quietly. "Even a yokel like me knows that."

"I never called you a yokel."

Abe sighed. "I know." He began fitting the boot and its mate into large plastic evidence baggies. "We'll see if the lab finds any traces of blood in the tread. If so, it won't matter how many other people have the same boots." Done with that, he looked up. "Ready to go check the boat's Starlink?"

Gray nodded mutely.

Both men shed their booties and crunched back out onto the tundra. Rounding the clapboard building, they approached the 20-foot cabin cruiser parked out back on a boat trailer. It was tightly sealed with a heavy-duty polyester tarp, which Abe immediately began loosening to grant access. Gray retrieved a stepstool from the shed and came back to find the cop trying—unsuccessfully—to rock the vessel on its rollers. When it didn't budge, he nodded. "Feels stable enough. All aboard."

Gray glanced under the snow-caked tarp and fumbled for his phone. It was quite dark outside at 7 in the morning here, but there was still ambient light from nearby buildings. Under that tarp, by contrast, it was pitch black. "You go first," Gray encouraged Abe instead, holding the ladder and lighting the enclosed space with his cell phone flashlight. "I don't want any question later whether I planted or tainted evidence."

"Fair enough."

Abe scrambled aboard and Gray followed, passing the cop Dawn's keychain. Soon they had the cabin unlocked, and they were greeted by the unique bouquet of syrupy antifreeze and tangy mildew as they stepped inside. "Here it is," Gray said, pointing at the small electronic device that was mounted above the steering wheel with bracket and screws. "May I?" By now, Gray had removed his thick winter gloves and donned a pair of latex like Abe, so the cop nodded—and Gray held down the Starlink's power button.

Nothing happened.

Abe started picking through several drawers, which already stood open. "Battery pack was probably removed when she winterized the boat... though from the smell, she didn't do a very thorough job of that. Ah, here it is," he said, finding the Starlink's power pack and reinstalling it.

"It looks like someone's been in here searching," Gray observed while they waited for the device to boot up. "*All* the drawers and cabinets are open."

"No, it's normal to leave them open," Abe assured him. "Helps with ventilation."

Once the Starlink was online, Abe started filming from his own phone as Gray thumbed through the user interface, tapping to open the trip history. September 13 wasn't the most recent entry, but it wasn't too far from the top either. Sure enough, Dawn had taken the boat out that day, into open water off the coast. As for the specific latitude and longitude...

"Damn," Gray whispered, comparing against the screenshots Samuel had sent him of the Dawn/David text exchange. "Coordinates match." Grasping at straws, he gave Abe a sidelong look. "How accurate are these things?"

"This is a pretty cheap model. I'd say accurate to fifty or a hundred feet. But still well within sight of any other boat at the exact coordinates."

"Then she simply made a mistake, arrived at the wrong time," Gray said doggedly. "Dawn insists she never saw David's boat."

Abe squinted at the little device's screen. "According to this, she was there twenty minutes before the murder, and she didn't leave until half an hour after. And remember, the device gets its timestamp from the satellite."

"So it's been tampered with," Gray shrugged.

The cop sighed. "It doesn't matter whether it has or not." He began digging in another open drawer for a screwdriver, preparing to remove the Starlink from its mounting to take into evidence. "You're forgetting, we've already got Dawn's fingerprints at the scene. Within the next few weeks, I imagine we'll have further confirmation from DNA and ballistics matches. Look, Gaynes, I don't want to believe it either, but we have to face the facts. Everything we've uncovered points unequivocally towards Dawn Simmonds as her brother's murderer."

"But what about motive?" Gray demanded. "Them being on the outs is hardly reason for murder."

"You know better than that. Besides, it could've been a heat-of-the-moment thing. Emotions can run hot where family is concerned."

"That's not how it plays in the video," Gray insisted. "Have you *seen* the video? Someone comes busting through the door and immediately shoots him. That feels more like premeditation."

"If it were truly premeditated," Abe countered, "why not switch to hollow points?"

Gray hesitated, because the cop made a valid argument. Everyone in NSB kept their handguns loaded with solid-metal bullets, or at least full metal jackets, for effective bear defense—to provide the depth of penetration needed to reach a bear's vital organs. But hollow points would be far preferable if the killer knew their target was human, because the way the bullets expanded and deformed on impact caused greater damage to soft human tissue while also making ballistics difficult. Instead, the killer had fired the kind of ammo that was probably always loaded by default... which suggested lack of planning, not premeditation at all.

"Maybe," Gray hedged. "But what about David Simmonds' last words about his big discovery, whatever it was that changed his understanding of what he'd been doing in the Arctic? Premeditated or not, *that* suggests the murder was related to his work, nothing to do with family."

"I don't know what to tell you, Gaynes," Abe said tiredly, then frowned. "Hey, what's that?"

Gray blinked. "What's... what?"

"That." He pointed past Gray to a pair of closed locker doors, where the cuff of a flannel shirt sleeve appeared to be poking out.

"What about it?" Gray tried the little door. "It's locked."

"Exactly. It should've been left open like the rest. And all clothing should be removed. Fabric's a breeding ground for mold. You have the key?"

Gray went through Dawn's keychain to find the right one, and soon he had the locker open. A pungent mustiness spread through the enclosed space, and Gray quickly raised his balaclava over mouth and nose. "I think we found our culprit," he said. "This shirt is covered with spores." He tried to pull it out. "Huh. It's wrapped around something." Moving carefully with his latex-gloved hands to avoid sending more mold into the air, he untied the shirtsleeves, then cursed and leaned back. Abe cursed even more colorfully when he saw.

Inside the flannel shirt was a brick of hard-packed white powder, its plastic packaging ripped open at one end.

"Drugs," Gray groaned.

"What do you think it is?" Abe asked. This was clearly way outside his experience. "Cocaine?"

"Maybe." Gray pointed. "But notice there's no mold growing on the powder, just the shirt? I would guess it's fentanyl. Unlike cocaine, that's a synthetic drug, meaning there'd be nothing organic for the mold to grow on. Besides, fentanyl's a much more lucrative business these days."

"But you don't know for sure. Can't you... I don't know... taste it?" Like cops were always doing in the movies, in other words.

Gray choked out a laugh. "If it *is* fentanyl, that would probably kill me. Even two milligrams can be a lethal dose. Besides, I think fentanyl's supposed to be tasteless anyway."

"Oh." Abe stared at the white powder for another long moment, then shook himself. "So what's it doing here?"

Gray's shoulders slowly slumped. "I don't know," he said, "but I can guess what we're meant to think."

"Meant to think?"

"By whoever planted this evidence."

Abe gave him a longsuffering look, but Gray pushed on. "We're meant to think Dawn was part of some drug smuggling operation David was running from Central America. After all, he took his yacht down that way every year, supposedly following whale migrations." Gray realized he probably shouldn't be airing these ideas to one of the very cops investigating Dawn's case; he still wasn't used to playing for the other team. But the NSBPD would hardly fail to arrive at the same theories soon enough anyway. "This is supposed to look like Dawn was the next step in the distribution pipeline once David got the drugs into the country."

"Despite the bad blood between them?"

Gray shrugged. "A prosecutor could argue that was all an act. To distract from the drug ring they were running together. Remember," he added hurriedly, "this is only what we're *meant* to think, not what I actually think." But inside, even Gray was starting to doubt a little.

"All that distance... sounds like an awful lot of trouble for just one bag of drugs," Abe said, nudging it. "Unless there's more?"

The two men quickly searched the rest of the boat, even shining a light into the bilge. After ten minutes, they concluded this was the only package of fentanyl—or whatever it was—on Dawn's cabin cruiser.

Still, even this one brick was nothing to sneeze at. Hefting it carefully so nothing spilled out the torn opening, Gray estimated it at five pounds—maybe two or three kilos. "Assuming they pressed this into pills..." He did some quick mental math. "Street value of this much powder could be as high as a million U.S."

"A million *dollars?*"

Gray nodded. "But I've been out of the game a while, so I could be way off."

"Still," Abe breathed, "with that kind of reward, maybe a single bag was worth the effort. Or maybe that's all they thought they could safely distribute. But why bring it *here* from Central America?"

"Because all the more likely trafficking vectors are carefully monitored. DEA, ATF, Coast Guard, you name it—they stop ships and do searches and frisk people coming into the country. I don't know all the details, especially these days," Gray admitted. "And obviously a lot still gets in, despite all efforts to the contrary. But smuggling drugs through the North Slope of Alaska probably isn't on anyone's radar."

"That's because it's stupid," Abe said flatly. "What would they do with the drugs once they got 'em here?"

"Oh, that's the easy part," Gray assured him. "Remember, you have hundreds of itinerant oil field workers—like me—flying in and out every two weeks. *Thousands*, when you count Deadhorse."

"But your bags are searched for contraband!"

"Only when we're coming *into* North Slope. Not so thoroughly when we're leaving."

The cop sat back on his heels, obviously still shocked at the ramifications of what they'd discovered.

"Cheer up, Abe, really," Gray said. "This is easy enough to counteract now that you know it's happening." He cocked his head. "Are you up for doing some more investigating?"

"Are you kidding?" the other man said, surprising Gray with a smile. "I feel bad for Dawn and her brother, but... honestly, this is the most exciting my job has ever been."

Gray laughed. "Great. Um... are you up for letting *me* tag along as you do more investigating?"

"What exactly did you have in mind?"

An hour later, they were sitting in matching seats before a big hardwood power desk in a modular building at the heart of TrephOil's U-Turn complex. The room itself was nothing special, interlocking wall panels and fluorescent lighting, but the desk was magnificent—its surface strategically arranged with knickknacks, awards, and framed photos alongside a computer monitor and keyboard. And centered precisely, facing the visitors, sat a wooden nameplate engraved with the most pretentious name Gray had ever encountered: Ptolemy D. Thrasher. No wonder everyone just called him Thrasher.

The company man, top-ranking official for Treadgold-Phelps Oil here in the North Slope, strode through the office door. “Abe, hey, sorry to keep you waiting.” Thrasher shook the cop’s hand before turning. “And you are—” He hesitated, obviously recognizing Gray even if Gray was incapable of returning the favor. “Wait, aren’t you one of my employees?”

Gray nodded respectfully and shook his boss’s boss’s boss’s hand. “Yes, sir, Gray Gaynes. At least, I work for you when I’m on hitch. Right now, I’m just a private investigator helping Dawn Simmonds.”

“Are you really.” Thrasher brightened. “Well, I’m glad someone is. Dawn and her restaurant do wonders for the morale of our people. That is to say,” he added quickly, “she’s a wonderful person, and I hope she’s cleared of all suspicion.” He sat back in his sumptuous leather desk chair and frowned suddenly, glancing between Abe and Gray. “But wait, you two are working together?”

“Not exactly, Mr. Thrasher,” Gray said, when Abe didn’t answer. “But that doesn’t mean we have to be adversarial.”

“We both just want the truth,” Abe agreed. “Which is why we’re here. We’re hoping you can help us with something.”

“Of course!” Thrasher enthused. “Anything for Dawn. And, um, the truth.”

"Great," Abe said, then dove right in. "Do you have any knowledge of an illegal drug smuggling operation going through U-Turn?"

Caught off guard, Thrasher gaped for a moment, one corner of his mouth twitching like he thought this might be a joke to laugh at. That stopped once he registered the serious expressions of the two investigators. "Noo," the company man said slowly, obviously still struggling to take this seriously. "Our men aren't even allowed to partake of alcohol in the NSB, much less recreational drugs."

"We're not asking about drug *use* in U-Turn," Gray clarified, "but drug *trafficking*."

"I have no knowledge of either," Thrasher said, leaning back in his chair and settling for an expression of faint amusement.

"Nor did I," Abe admitted, "until today." When the company man continued to eye him skeptically, the cop sighed. "Well, do you have any employees with past record of such involvement?"

Thrasher blinked. "I... well, maybe I do." He shrugged. "These are rough men, as you yourself know." His eyes flicked to Gray apologetically. "Some of them, at least." He turned back to Abe. "But even if some of my people have a record, I'm sure that life is far behind them."

"Maybe it is," Abe agreed, "but we still have to look into anyone like that." He and Gray had discussed this on the way over, the fact that anyone involved in street-level distribution down south would probably have a record. Abe gestured toward Thrasher's curved ultrawide computer monitor. "Mind running a search, giving us the names of any employees whose background checks flagged a criminal record?"

Thrasher finally did laugh out loud. "Of course I mind! I mean, I'd love to help—and will help—but not without a warrant."

Gray spoke up. "But this is for Dawn."

Thrasher frowned. "I don't see how."

Gray exchanged glances with Abe, whose eyes cautioned him not to divulge too much. "Let's just say, if there *is* a drug operation going on here, the murder of Dawn's brother was probably related to that. The best way to clear Dawn's name is to catch the people who were really responsible." Gray only hoped those same people didn't implicate Dawn in turn, as Abe probably expected.

Thrasher gazed thoughtfully at Gray for a long moment before he nodded. Turning toward his widescreen display, he punched a few commands on his keyboard, searched, scrolled, and punched some more. But eventually he sat back, looking a little surprised and more than a little displeased. Then, abruptly, he stood. "I'm gonna go grab some coffee." And he left the room.

Abe furrowed his brow at Gray, mystified. "What's that all about?"

Gray snorted. "He's seen too many movies." The former NYPD detective stood, began moving around the power desk, then paused and spoke quietly. "Still, if we look at this screen, you won't be able to use any of this information in court. I'm not just talking about Dawn's trial here. I'm talking about anyone you arrest on drug charges too." He cocked his head. "Are you okay with that?"

Abe looked uneasy, but he shrugged. "If we catch someone smuggling drugs through U-Turn, we'll obviously end up running their record on our own. But we'll never catch them in the first place if we don't know who to look into."

That kind of logic made for a slippery slope, and something deep within Gray recoiled at cutting corners like this. But helping Dawn was more important, and he didn't have time for bureaucratic delays. So he nodded and finished rounding the desk, sitting down before Thrasher's screen.

There were five search results displayed there, five TrephOil employees with past convictions on drug-related charges. Surely this wasn't *all* the ex-cons in TrephOil's employ, but Thrasher was apparently savvy enough with his search parameters to include just the most relevant results.

Raising his phone, Gray snapped a couple quick photos of the information. He started to rise, then hesitated. There would never be a better opportunity to search TrephOil's records for any Dons operating out of U-Turn—there may never be *any* other opportunity, based on Thrasher's reticence just now—and Gray needed that info, since borough tax records only extended to full-time residents. So Gray ignored his increasingly beleaguered conscience and leaned forward, finding the search filter textbox and typing DAWN. But there were no results.

"What are you doing?" Abe asked suspiciously.

"Just checking for any other possible suspects," Gray said, which was true enough. But then, why did he feel the blood rush to his face?

Still, Gray searched for DON next. This time, he hit pay dirt. There were eight employees in the history of TrephOil's North Slope operations for whom D-O-N appeared in the first, middle, or last name somewhere. Gray quickly snapped more photos of their information too, then cleared his search.

And that was that. Abe, despite his verbal blessing on this escapade, never even stood from his chair. He was obviously second-guessing himself, which was just as well.

"C'mon," Gray said evenly. "I've become aware of some information that might have bearing on your efforts to keep U-Turn drug-free." Gray's new list of alternate Dons would have to wait.

Abe Kanayurak sighed, but he rose and followed Gray quietly out of Thrasher's office.

The first roustabout from Thrasher's initial search results—ex-cons with past drug convictions—was one Larry-Jean Higgen... and he would prove to be the very man Abe and Gray were looking for. When did *that* ever happen?

The fellow was on night shift this hitch and it was now past 9 a.m., meaning Higgen was probably thinking about bed if he wasn't there already. After a few minutes' discussion, Abe opted to return to his substation to tackle some unrelated paperwork while Gray did preliminary investigation at Higgen's dorm. They didn't yet know Higgen was their guy, of course; he was simply the first man on the list.

The P.I. knocked quietly on a few neighboring doors to start, interviewing oil field workers housed on the same hall as Higgen. Since TrephOil tended to billet members of the same crew in proximity to each other, this was a good way to find the men who knew Higgen best. Most weren't happy to be roused at this hour, and several ignored Gray's knock entirely; but he spoke with enough of them. He started by proffering his business card and explaining that he was investigating a drug smuggling operation—

which was enough to wake them up fully. Then Gray just asked if they knew anyone who might be involved. All he needed was one person who was already aware of Higgen's past... and eventually, one old roughneck obliged. "Ha," the man snorted, "if anyone's smuggling drugs, it's prolly Larry-Jean Higgen."

The man was only being half serious. Still, Gray could now honestly tell Abe—and did so, with a quick phone call—that Higgen's coworkers had volunteered his name in connection with possible drug trafficking. It wasn't honest at all, of course. If Gray had still been a cop himself, this would've been unethical in the extreme. Whatever Higgen's past, Gray hardly knew (yet) if he was guilty of new crimes, but he was practically inviting the man's colleagues to drag his name through the mud—making it all the harder for the fellow to reintegrate with law-abiding society, if that was his aim. And yet legally, at least, Gray had covered his bases; this was a gray area since he was snooping around as a private investigator, then passing his suspicions along to the NSBPD as a tip. And besides, he reminded himself, this all served a higher purpose: clearing the name of a woman he still considered a true innocent, someone who (unlike Higgen) had *never* actually committed a crime. Anyway, what mattered was that Abe Kanayurak—himself an active, sworn officer of the law—was protected. The cop now had a legitimate reason for standing at Larry-Jean Higgen's door and knocking to ask about drugs. And if Higgen was uninvolved, no harm, no foul. Right?

Higgen was not innocent.

Despite the hour, Abe and Gray had an audience when the cop's knuckles wrapped on the dorm room door, a half dozen other TrephOil employees standing in their own doorways. And since Abe had alerted company security as a professional courtesy, one of their own officers stood at the ready as well—a friendly giant named Harmon Freyes who was dressed head to toe in snow camo fatigues, complete with the three-leaf logo of Treadgold-Phelps Oil emblazoned on a shoulder patch. What's more, Freyes carried a 10mm Glock 20 securely holstered on one hip, since security personnel were the *only* company personnel allowed to bear arms.

When Higgen darkened his own door, Gray took an involuntary step back. The guy was easily 6'-6" and all muscle—bigger even than Freyes. "Larry-Jean Higgen?" Abe began. "We'd like to talk to you about two kilos of drugs we recovered from—"

The brute's balled fist came out of nowhere, catapulting Abe into the corridor's opposite wall, even as the man's other fist took Gray in the groin. The P.I. doubled over, gasping for air, as Higgen dashed past—but the roustabout didn't make it halfway down the hall before Freyes slammed him into a wall, then laid him out cold on the floor. The security officer had the man's wrists bound in heavy nylon zip ties long before he began stirring again.

"Damn," Abe moaned, feeling at his chin. "I think he broke my jaw."

"I'm gonna be peeing blood for a week," Gray rejoined.

To Abe's credit, he was back on his feet in moments and stumbling down the hall. He had to wait until the fellow woke before reading him his rights, however. After that, Abe and Freyes each took an arm to drag Higgen to the holding cell at U-Turn's NSBPD substation.

The company doctor—a man named Douglass who wore the strangest square-framed spectacles Gray had ever seen—met them there. He cared for a cut on Higgen's cheek before they locked him up, then turned to Abe and Gray, eventually clearing both men of serious injury.

"I guess that paid off," Abe told Gray cheerfully, a deep bruise discoloring one side of his face below the cheek.

"I'm not so sure it was worth it," Gray grumbled, moving gingerly. The two of them stood at the substation's entrance after seeing Douglass and Freyes off, out of sight from their new suspect.

"But there's no question this guy's involved," Abe said quietly.

Gray agreed. "Want to take a run at him? See if he'll tell us anything without a lawyer present?"

Abe looked amused at Gray's use of 'us.' "Sure, but let me turn on the camera and loop in Jameson.

As for you... you better stay out of the shot, and keep silent."

"I get it," Gray agreed. "I'm not officially here."

Soon enough, Detectives Jameson and Aiken were conferenced in from Utqiaġvik, their voices audible over Abe's office speakerphone. NSBPD headquarters already had an audiovisual uplink from U-Turn's holding cell via the security camera mounted above Abe's desk, though it was generally only activated and monitored when the cell was occupied overnight.

And sobbing, Higgen began to talk quite freely, confessing everything outright—despite his lack of an attorney or plea deal.

"Each hitch," the man sniffled, "the last night before we fly home, I scoop some ivory into my steel-toes."

"Ivory?" Abe asked, confused.

"Yeah, man, King Ivory." When the cop still looked confused, Higgen tried, "White ladies? The gray stuff?" He sighed. "I mean *fetty*, man." These were obviously all street names for fentanyl; Gray had been right.

Jameson's voice came over the speaker. "*I want to be sure I understand, Mr. Higgen. You're saying that you scoop powdered fentanyl into your work boots, which you then wear through the airport to smuggle back to Anchorage?*"

"Exactly," Higgen said, actually giving a tremulous smile, happy to be understood. "Even if someone sees it, it looks like snow, y'know?"

This guy is an idiot, Gray thought to himself. He had just brought another federal charge onto his head by admitting he carried illegal drugs through an airport. Then again, Higgen's obvious relief put his confession in a different light. No matter his tendency toward breaking the law, here was a man forever burdened with a desperate need to clear his guilty conscience. Gray had been blessed to know a few others of this sort, if only a few, back during his NYPD career.

"*How much fentanyl?*" Jameson wanted to know.

"Huh?"

"*How much fetty do you scoop into your work boots before each flight home?*"

"Oh!" The roustabout's expression cleared. "Like, a cup in each."

"As in a measuring cup's worth or a larger drinking cup?" Abe asked. "Eight ounces or..." He trailed off at Higgen's bewildered look.

"*What happens when you get to Anchorage?*" Jameson spoke up again.

Higgen shrugged. "I go home."

"*Which is where?*"

"I got a place in Muldoon." That was a neighborhood in Anchorage, Gray knew. "Leave my boots in the mudroom, with the back door unlocked. Next morning, I find a brand-new pair of boots in their place—same brand and all—with a knot in one toe."

Abe was bewildered again. "Sorry, a knot?"

Higgen sighed in exasperation, wiping some fresh moisture from his eyes. "Cash, man, a whole fat wad of it."

As Higgen talked more, Gray quickly realized the whole operation was as unsophisticated as they came. Sure, loose white grit in a man's shoe wouldn't raise anyone's suspicions—though obviously, no one would think it was *snow*, or it would have melted—and transporting even so little would be highly profitable. Heck, a single ounce of the stuff in powdered form had a street value north of ten grand. But if law enforcement in Anchorage ever did begin to suspect (as they probably would from here on out), the addition of just one narcotic detection dog stationed at the airport would bring this kind of scheme crashing to the ground.

From the way Abe's lip curled, he was clearly more disgusted at the prospect of ingesting drugs that had seen the inside of a sweaty work boot. But that was hardly the most unsanitary place drugs might be smuggled, and certainly where fentanyl was concerned, hygiene was the least of the dangers.

"*How long have you been doing this?*" a new voice asked, probably Aiken, the other detective linked in from Utqiaġvik.

"As long as I've been with the company," Higgen admitted, which set off a fresh round of racking sobs. They had to wait until he calmed again before continuing.

"*And who are you working with?*"

"I don't know who takes my shoes in Muldoon."

"*In U-Turn, though. Who do you get the drugs from* here?"

Higgen only hesitated a moment before giving in to his conscience. "That Native lady which owns the restaurant. The one with the tats on her face." He snapped his fingers. "Dawn something."

Abe slowly turned to meet Gray's eyes, his expression apologetic.

Gray had a half dozen angry questions he wanted to ask this suspect, and he immediately began texting the first one to Abe in hopes that *he* would ask. Gray didn't believe for a minute that Higgen was working with Dawn to smuggle drugs into the United States. At the same time, having just sat through this very awkward and emotional interrogation, Gray did not doubt that Larry-Jean Higgen believed every word of his own confession. And unfortunately, that meant the cops *and* a jury would believe it too.

Dawn Simmonds was now an accused drug smuggler in addition to murderer. Things just kept going from bad to worse.

The next two weeks,
December 27th – January 8th

U-Turn

"I'm sorry," the normally mild Samuel Leavitt demanded incredulously over the phone. *"Say that one more time?"*

"They're adding charges of drug trafficking and distribution to first degree murder on Dawn's criminal complaint," Gray repeated tiredly.

Samuel laughed a little hysterically. *"Oh, is that all?"*

"Well... no. Importation of controlled substances too, and conspiracy for good measure," Gray added a little hoarsely.

Samuel's laughter was short-lived. *"And all because you helped identify and arrest some low-level druggie, and that guy implicated Dawn."*

Gray squirmed. "Yes."

"Are you trying *to make things worse for our client?"*

The silence that ensued was long and awkward. Gray had said from the beginning that he would follow the facts of this case wherever they led; but this latest discovery *did* make Samuel's job much harder, so he could hardly be blamed for lashing out. Gray was cursing himself too, though he hardly knew what he could have done differently.

It was now evening on the day of Higgen's arrest. The drug mule's interrogation had continued through much of the afternoon, across multiple sessions. In between, Abe had returned to Dawn's place for another careful search. Gray had not been invited.

"*And what do you think of this man's testimony?*" Samuel finally asked. "*Will he be difficult to discredit in court?*"

Gray sighed. "He's not the brightest crayon in the box, so I think it'd be obvious if he was lying. *He* at least believes what he's saying."

"*And what is he alleging, exactly?*"

"He says Dawn first contacted him by phone—voice call—asking if he was interested in, quote, 'moving some ivory,' end-quote. Ivory is street slang for fentanyl."

"*And in this phone call, she actually identified herself as Dawn Simmonds?*" Samuel clarified.

"No."

"*Too bad. Even a jury would've found that hard to believe.*" Pause. "*So how did this Larry-Jean Higgen know it was Dawn?*"

"I'm getting to that," Gray assured him. "Anyway, they talked several times that week by phone, negotiating price until he was willing to take the risk. Then the woman on the other end of the line told him where to find the drugs." Gray took a deep breath. "In Dawn's boat."

"*Which was parked in Dawn's backyard,*" Samuel said sourly. "*The same place you and Abe found the two-kilo brick of remaining fentanyl.*"

"Correct."

"*From which he concluded the woman on the phone must be Dawn. Which... most juries will agree is a reasonable assumption.*"

"Right."

Samuel grumbled something indecipherable. "*But,*" he asked after a moment, "*the woman never sent Higgen any emails or text messages?*"

"So he says."

"*Meaning there's no actual evidence of their conversation.*" The lawyer paused. "*And they never met in person? If not, I can probably lead him to doubting his own confidence in the woman's identity, once I get him on the stand.*"

"Well... he and Dawn *did* interact in person on a few occasions when Higgen ate at Dawn's place," Gray said slowly. "And from what he says, they spoke... obliquely... about their arrangement. Winks and nods and so forth." Gray shook his head. "The whole thing probably left Dawn bewildered, but

Higgen thinks there was a meaningful subtext going on. Trying to convince him otherwise might be difficult."

Samuel groaned. "*And of course there are probably other oil field workers who can attest to seeing them together. I'll ask Dawn what she remembers of their conversations—heck, if she even remembers Higgen—but it probably doesn't matter. Anything she says will be suspect to a jury.*" The lawyer thought for a moment. "*How did she supposedly identify Higgen as a potential mule in the first place?*"

"That's exactly what I wanted to know," Gray said. "Some of Higgen's coworkers knew he'd done time for low-level distribution. Jameson theorizes Dawn overheard them gossiping about it when they came in to eat, but I don't buy it. Overhearing vague gossip, sure, but enough specifics for her to act on it? It's not like she would have stopped the workers mid-rumor and asked for the name and number of the man they were gossiping about."

"*It does seem unlikely,*" Samuel agreed. "*But I hate to make that assumption. The way this case is going, the cops will probably find some driller's assistant willing to testify that's exactly what she did.*"

"Want me to go back and interview his coworkers again, make sure that's—"

"*No,*" Samuel cut in vehemently. "*Let the cops uncover their own damning evidence from now on.*"

Pause. "*So the boat was the drop point for the drugs?*"

"Higgen would sneak under the tarp during off hours—when Dawn's place was closed—and unlock the cabinet to get at them, yeah. Says she left spare keys on the boat that very first time, and indeed, Abe found those keys still on the man's keychain."

"*And how long have they supposedly had this arrangement? Dawn and Higgen?*"

"As long as Higgen's been working for TrephOil."

"*Which is how long?*" Samuel pressed.

"That's the thing," Gray said. "This is only Higgen's first season. Suggesting this all started *after* David was murdered, maybe six weeks ago."

"*That's... not what I was expecting to hear.*" The lawyer was silent for a moment. "*How did Dawn get paid in this arrangement?*" Samuel wanted to know, belatedly adding: "*Supposedly.*"

"That part is still unexplained. Some third party would pay Higgen once he got back to Anchorage—just his fee for being the courier. We're not sure how Dawn supposedly got her cut, but..." Gray sighed. He felt like he'd been doing that a lot lately. "But Abe did go back to Dawn's today for a more thorough search, this time looking for places she might have hidden money. And sure enough, he confiscated about fifty thousand dollars in weathered bills that were stuffed into envelopes in her mattress."

"*Of course he did. Do you have any other good news for me?*"

"Well, I accessed the Starlink on Dawn's cabin cruiser like you requested. The trip history confirms she *was* at the rendezvous at the right time and place for the murder. No mistake."

"*Great,*" Samuel groused. "*So much for that.*"

"And there's the boots too," Gray remembered suddenly, telling Samuel about the bloody boot print the cops had photographed at the crime scene, which Abe had matched to the tread pattern of Dawn's own boots. "Abe ran a blacklight over them before I left his substation tonight." Gray rubbed his forehead. "It turned up blood in the tread."

Samuel swore.

"Of course, they still have to test it," Gray went on, "which will take weeks—just like the other DNA and ballistics evidence. But I don't doubt it'll come back as a match for David Simmonds."

Samuel was quiet a moment. "*Does this mean even you have started doubting Dawn's innocence?*"

"No, I'm just being a pessimist," Gray said darkly. "Everything else so cleanly points to her guilt. I'm sure this will too." He shook his head. "I'm more sure than ever this is a frame job."

Samuel pointedly said nothing for a long moment. Then: "*I leave you to uncover that proof. Just try not to damage our case any further in the process,*" he concluded cooly.

Gray stayed Wednesday night at Ephron's again. And in the morning, despite Samuel's warnings, he sought out the old roughneck from Larry-Jean Higgen's crew—the same man who had implicated Higgen when Gray knocked on his door the day before. Gray was waiting at the man's dorm room when he got home from night shift Thursday a.m., and after a quick shower, the old codger invited Gray down to the cafeteria with him.

"Jim Bing," he introduced himself, friendly enough. "And 'course I knew 'bout Larry-Jean's past," the old fella said while stuffing a forkful of steaming flapjacks into his mouth, adding half a sausage link for good measure and chasing it all down with a slurp of scalding coffee. "We all did."

"How so?"

"Idiot told us, that very first hitch. These young'uns like to brag, you know, prove which of 'em's a badder dude. All the new roustabouts went around the circle, posturin'." Bing glanced over Gray's stained coveralls—still the warmest thing he had to wear each day—and correctly concluded he was on a drilling crew himself. "You know how it is. Lots of the guys have a past."

Gray nodded. "Where did you discuss this? On the bus? On the drill floor?"

"Nah, over dinner."

Gray felt a sinking sensation. "Here at the dining hall?"

The old guy's weathered face creased in thought. "Nah, up at that Eskimo girl's place."

"Iñupiaq," Gray corrected him automatically. "Or just Inuit. 'Eskimo' can be offensive, not a word the Native Alaskans ever used for themselves." It was something he'd repeated many times to the other workers since learning it from Dawn himself, his first season on the slope.

"Really?" The roughneck raised an apologetic hand. "I didn't mean no disrespect."

But Gray's mind was already spinning through the implications. Higgen had actually bragged of his criminal past in Dawn's hearing, and Gray had to assume the cops would learn of it as easily as he had. The prosecution would go on to argue that Dawn accepted all modern forms of payment at her restaurant... and if Higgen, as a paying customer, ever opted to get his receipt via text message, Dawn would've known his phone number. They didn't have to prove this *had* happened, only that it could have—and just like that, the idea of Dawn recruiting a drug mule went from farfetched to feasible.

Of course, Gray knew that anyone else at Dawn's place that night could have overheard the same conversation, then sought out Higgen's phone number a different way. But that wouldn't be enough to counteract the picture the prosecution would paint.

The private investigator thanked Mr. Bing and tried not to act as though there was anything earth-shattering in the man's testimony. Maybe he'd get lucky and the cops never would find this thread... a hope that faded when Gray passed Abe coming into the dining hall as he was leaving. The uniformed cop made a beeline for Jim Bing.

Gray spent the afternoon and evening looking into the new list of Dons he'd identified from Thrasher's computer. None of the eight names were familiar to him, and he saw now that most of them were inactive records (former employees who'd resigned or been terminated more than a year earlier). That left only two Dons employed by TrephOil at the time of the murder, and both were roughnecks, meaning neither man had been in the North Slope—because September was squarely in the off season, when drilling operations were significantly reduced. Ah well, it had been a long shot anyway.

On Friday, Ephron gave Gray a lift to TrephOil's airstrip on his late model snow machine. There, Gray boarded Jacob's bush plane with plans to complete his circuit of the North Slope over the next five days, ringing in the New Year while interviewing the rest of the alternate Dons. Jacob was kind enough to wait an hour in Kaktovik while Gray ran down one name there, then dropped him in Deadhorse at lunchtime. Servicing Prudhoe Bay, Deadhorse was the largest work camp on the slope, ten times the size of U-Turn. Gray easily could have kept busy for a week chasing down Dons here... except it would've proven an even bigger waste of time than it was in U-Turn. It was only the maintenance, planning, and construction crews who were on-site during the off season, and Gray learned as much as he needed about *those* Deadhorse Dons with what remained of the weekend. None stood out as viable suspects.

And Sunday night—New Year's Eve—all of Gray's exhaustion finally caught up with him. Returning to his hotel as the last smudge of twilight faded, Gray collapsed into bed and was asleep by 4 p.m. He never even stirred as the rest of Deadhorse rang in the New Year some eight hours later.

Monday morning—New Year's Day—Gray turned down an offer to accompany one ice road trucker 400 miles south along the Dalton Highway towards Fairbanks. Not only did the thought of *days* traveling an ice road terrify him; it didn't even get him that close to Anaktuvuk Pass, a mountain village of 400 where he'd originally hoped to interview another Don. By now, Gray had exhausted all of NSB's most likely suspects, leaving only the Dons far outside of David Simmonds' summer stomping grounds—250 miles south of the Arctic coast in Anaktuvuk Pass, or 100 to 300 miles southwest of Utqiaġvik in Wainwright, Point Lay, or Point Hope. And despite more than twelve hours of blissful oblivion the night before, Gray remained exhausted, so... he finally let himself off the hook. The rest of his persons of interest, all highly unlikely and thus not really that interesting, he interviewed by phone. And on Tuesday afternoon, Jacob flew him back to U-Turn from Deadhorse on his normal mail run.

It was a thoroughly exhausted and demoralized Grayson Gaynes, TrephOil roughneck 'fifth hand,' who boarded the bus to the drill site at 6 a.m. on Wednesday morning—now officially back on-hitch after two weeks of failing to uncover any alternative suspects or theories in the murder of David Simmonds. Gray's crew seemed to have forgotten all about his episode arriving late to work that one time last hitch, and no one had missed him on the flights to and from Anchorage. Motormouth Miller and the rest were in high spirits, friendly and boisterous after weeks resting and celebrating the holidays. Of all the crew, Gray alone was surly, having pushed himself past the point of exhaustion for four straight weeks—and having another two weeks of grueling work in subzero temps to look forward to, starting today. Gray's only saving grace was that this hitch, his crew was on day shift. He didn't even have a homecooked dinner at Dawn's place to look forward to after shift each day.

The days that followed quickly blurred together, and Gray knew he was dangerously close to burnout, notwithstanding his single good night's sleep on New Year's Eve. Aside from the work itself, Gray spent every evening going through more video log entries, from the time he stumbled through the door of his dorm room to the moment his eyes finally refused commands to stay open. And still, he uncovered nothing. Gray continued to worry he was missing something important, either due to ignorance or exhaustion—just as he worried that one of the many Dons he'd interviewed these last weeks was, in fact, the true killer, despite giving Gray no cause for suspicion at the time. And with all this stress upon him, what sleep Gray *did* manage started to suffer, his hours of semiconscious 'rest' filled with nonsensical nightmares.

Then came Samuel's phone call, as Gray was trudging home from work the next Monday. The call that put the nail in the coffin of Dawn's defense.

"*Expedited results are back from the state police lab,*" the lawyer said without preamble. "*DNA, ballistics, the whole nine.*"

Gray found a parked work truck to sag against. He could already tell from Samuel's tone of voice what those results must be.

"*Hair and skin samples found at the scene match Dawn Simmonds. Blood recovered from the tread of Dawn's boot matches the victim, David Simmonds. And ballistics confirm he was killed by Dawn's Ruger Super Redhawk, no doubt about it.*"

Gray squeezed his eyes shut, though of course he wasn't surprised.

"*I have a visit with her later today,*" Samuel concluded. "*I'm going to advise her to take a plea. I think I can argue that the drugs were opportunistic, at least; that she found the fentanyl only after David was dead. Should be enough to get her out of the importation and conspiracy charges, anyway.*"

Gray didn't remind Samuel that the prosecution would now offer less incentive for any plea deal. With all the evidence in, the state's case against Dawn had become a slam dunk.

"*Well?*" the lawyer pressed. "*Don't you have anything to say?*"

"Only that this is obviously a frame job," Gray replied tiredly. "It's more obvious now than ever."

Samuel sighed. "*I want to believe that too, but I have to be realistic.*"

"Look," Gray said, ticking points off on his gloved fingers as his breath billowed into the frigid air before him. "Dawn had three months to dispose of those bloody boots. If she really was the killer, and she was capable of all these other things she's being accused of, then she'd be too smart not to burn everything she was wearing when she murdered David—boots included. The only reason she didn't dispose of the boots is because she didn't know she needed to."

"*But Gray—*"

"And again, the way she supposedly deleted the text exchange between herself and the victim, instead of just setting her messages to expire after a month? Plus her Starlink puts her at the scene of the crime at time of death. If she was smart enough to turn off location services on her phone, why not throw the Starlink overboard after doing the deed?"

"*All good questions,*" Samuel admitted. "*None of which invalidate the clear evidence against her.*"

"DNA can be planted," Gray pointed out.

"*And ballistics?*"

"You know better than me there's no registration or permit required to carry a handgun in Alaska. No documentation of private sales either."

"*But why does that matter,*" Samuel asked, "*when the murder weapon was found on her person?*"

"Because no one can prove that Dawn is the one who purchased *that* weapon. Think about it. Dawn purchased *a* Ruger Super Redhawk at some point, years ago," Gray said. "But without documentation, there's no way to prove that's the same weapon the cops pulled out of her holster when they arrested her. What if someone else murdered David Simmonds with the same kind of gun—it's a very common model, after all—then switched the murder weapon with Dawn's? I don't know, broke into her place and did it while she was sleeping maybe, sometime in the last three months. There's no reason she ever would have noticed."

Samuel was thoughtful a moment. "*And unless she herself kept documentation of the original purchase, you're right—she couldn't prove now that this one wasn't always hers. Okay, I'll ask when I see her. Maybe she wrote down the gun's serial number, at least. But Gray...*"

"I know, I know. It still wouldn't prove anything. The evidence against her is pretty staggering." Gray paused, examining his own motives, knowing he wasn't as confident in Dawn's innocence as he pretended. "It's just... if she *is* the killer, she's jumped back and forth too much between smart and stupid moves. The gun is just another example of this. She could have dumped it *and* the Starlink, and just replaced them. Why didn't she? The most satisfying explanation is that someone else is trying to make Dawn look as guilty as possible."

"*But why would anyone else go to all this trouble framing her?*" Samuel asked quietly. "*And what was their motive for murdering David in the first place*?"

"I have no idea," Gray confessed.

There was a moment of silence. "*You know I still want to believe in Dawn too,* do *still believe in her,*" Samuel reiterated in a calm tone. "*But given the preponderance of damaging evidence, I'm losing hope we can convince a jury. You still haven't found any actual proof she was framed. And I have an ethical obligation to counsel Dawn realistically, which in this case means—*"

"Advising she take a plea deal, rather than risking life in prison if she's convicted at trial." Gray sighed. "I understand." And he really did. Samuel hadn't lost faith in Dawn so much as in an imperfect justice system. "I have just one request."

"*What's that?*"

"Call me when you're with Dawn later, during your visit. A video call, preferably. I have a question I need to ask her face to face."

"*Okay. It'll be an hour or two.*"

The men chatted a little longer, but there wasn't much more to be said. They hung up soon after, and Gray managed to sneak a shower, then text Ephron to make other arrangements before his phone rang again. Glancing at the caller ID, Gray accepted the call.

Dawn's face appeared on his screen—her tattoos familiar, the face beneath unrecognizably haggard, devoid of warmth and hope. Samuel had already told her the bad news.

"Did you keep any documentation when you bought your gun? The Ruger?" Gray asked.

She shook her head, looking confused. "*No. That's what you needed to ask me, face to face?*"

"Not really." Gray took a deep breath. "Dawn... did you murder your brother?"

She recoiled. "*No! I told you I didn't!*"

"Did you stick your revolver in his face and blow it half off?" Gray pressed mercilessly. "Did you splatter your brother's brains all over the wall of his yacht?"

"*What?! No!*" Dawn was sobbing now. "*I promise— I didn't— I—*" she stumbled over her own tongue, voice thick with horror, even as Samuel said something angry in the background. "*How— why would you—*"

And through the protestations, Gray studied her. Her reaction was hardly conclusive. Even murderers got emotional sometimes, honestly horrified when confronted with reminders of their dark deeds. Still, Gray decided he believed her, despite all new evidence to the contrary. He was hardly confident; he questioned his own intuition these days and probably always would, but he chose to trust it in this moment anyway... chose to trust *her*. He supposed that was the nature of faith sometimes, acting despite doubt.

And in this case, the time had come for action.

"I'm sorry," he told her, gentle now. "I just needed you to reassure me. Before..."

"*Before what?*" she asked, wiping moisture from her eyes.

"Before I do something... rash."

Tuesday, January 9th

The Beaufort Sea,

70°52'30.0"N 151°01'45.7"W

Gray blew off work the next morning. Oh, he called in to HR, told them he wouldn't be able to make it, but he didn't give an excuse. Gray wasn't sick today, after all, just crazy.

His second call was to Detective Jameson. "*I guess you heard the news?*" the cop asked after answering. Remarkably, he didn't seem to be gloating. "*DNA and ballistics match.*"

"I heard. I would like to visit the crime scene," Gray replied evenly. "Would you please arrange me transport to David Simmonds' yacht with NSB Search & Rescue?"

Jameson scoffed, of course. "*We're not flying you out there.*"

"As an investigator for the defense, I am entitled to see the crime scene for myself."

"*And you will,*" Jameson assured him gruffly. "*Once the ice thaws and we tow the crime scene back to shore.*"

"I'll happily wait and go with your officers the next time NSBPD returns to the scene, but I can't wait until spring."

"*Well, we're not going back before then, and neither are the troopers.*" Jameson meant the state troopers, including the ABI—Alaska's state-level version of the FBI. "*We've gathered all the evidence we need, and crime lab results are conclusive. Any return trips are a waste of taxpayer dollars.*"

Gray smiled tightly, carefully transcribing the entire conversation, word for word, for future reference. The NSBPD detective had effectively said that law enforcement had finished their work and released the scene. And while Jameson probably didn't want Gray poking around the yacht unsupervised, he hadn't explicitly said so; he only refused to provide transportation to and from.

The private investigator swallowed. Part of him had hoped the cop would outright forbid him from going. But of course, Jameson probably didn't think he needed to. Gray would indeed be crazy to attempt such a thing by himself. But that was a risk he would have to take. All he'd needed was Dawn's reassurance that she was worth that risk.

So, as soon as he hung up with the detective, Gray set out. Just him and the snow machine he'd borrowed from Ephron, laden with food, supplies, gasoline, and an emergency beacon—just in case.

He avoided the main snow road that connected U-Turn with the outside world, though that would have saved him a little time from the start. TrephOil had security personnel like Harmon Freyes stationed at the turnoff to each active drill site, and while Gray wasn't doing anything wrong—aside from playing hooky—he didn't want to draw attention or questions. Nor did he want to risk catching Abe Kanayurak's eye. He would be taking enough risks today as it was; so instead, he drove ten miles due south, then banked wide east before continuing north and opening the throttle.

To about 15 mph—even slower than when Jeannette showed him the ropes. He wasn't an experienced driver like the locals and, again, didn't want to take unnecessary risks. Besides, this had been a relatively low snow year thus far, providing too little packed snow base for comfortable operation at speed.

All told, it took Gray more than four hours to reach the coast, where he stopped for the first time, refueling from one of the extra cans on the snow machine's luggage rack. The journey thus far had been just short of miserable, trying to stay awake and alert while huddled behind the snowmobile's windshield, but the machine's heated seat and the hand and thumb warmers integrated into its handlebars—made the trip bearable. Grateful though he was to stretch his back, Gray eagerly returned to those meager sources of warmth as soon as the gas can was secure once more.

And resuming his journey, he *really* started taking his time. Easing out onto the ice of the

Beaufort Sea, he crept along for the first mile or two, heart in his throat—for the ice made *noise*.

The creaking and cracking and popping he had expected, though not the fear it inspired within him. So far as Gray could see and feel, the snow-clad ice of the ocean surface remained stable beneath his vehicle, but the *sound* of the snowmobile's passage played tricks on his equilibrium—convincing him the ice was about to give way. Then came the first eerie wail in the distance, unnatural, punctuated by a sudden resonant boom.

A gunshot? Was someone shooting at him?

No, these were just more of the noises ice might make when floes rubbed or crashed against each other. Ephron had warned him, even as he'd shaken his head at Gray's foolhardiness. It had been a warm year, and just as the snow was thin, so was the ice—maybe four inches, Ephron estimated, not the six to eight he preferred for safe snowmobile operation. The big Iñupiaq man had given Gray one chance in ten of going in the drink, which was why Gray was taking it so slow this close to shore... and why Ephron had insisted on $8,000 collateral before handing over his keys. Gray had grudgingly written a personal check.

Of course, at this point, it probably didn't matter if Gray was five feet from land or five miles. If he went through the ice and got wet in these temperatures, he was a dead man unless he found immediate shelter. The best way to minimize that danger was to reduce the amount of *time* he spent on the ice. So he cautiously accelerated back to his previous speed and let Ephron's GPS guide him to David Simmonds' boat.

When the yacht emerged from the gloom some three hours later, Gray finally understood why this boat was such a big deal to everyone. None of the crime scene photos had done it justice, having mostly been taken onboard, with only a few outside shots taken from the air.

First off, the boat was immense as private vessels went—three times the length of Dawn's cabin cruiser, but also wider and taller. Hell, this thing had three complete decks above the level of the ice, complete with cushioned lounge areas for passengers to sun themselves in milder climes. Sporting sharp lines and a flybridge festooned with antennae and satellite dishes, the whole of it still seeming shiny and new under its coat of bright white paint... this vessel had been luxurious even before David's aftermarket retrofits, which made it possible for him to operate in arctic waters with a crew of just one. Gray admittedly knew little of nautical matters, but he knew this much:

This was a multimillion-dollar extravagance that made all the local watercraft look outdated and beggarly by comparison.

And yet, the yacht also appeared ghostly in the dark, stuck fast in the ice with not a single light glowing. If Gray hadn't been so thoroughly chilled by eight hours of riding through subzero temps, he might have hesitated. Instead, he did a single loop of the ghost ship before bringing his borrowed snow machine alongside the stern of the vessel. There, he shut off his engine for the first time, tying off the snowmobile to one of the boat's stainless steel mooring cleats.

And then he shivered, as much from the sudden relative silence as the bone-deep cold. This was, Gray abruptly realized, the most alone he had ever been.

Fumbling with the first of his packs, Gray located Ephron's little extreme action video camera and connected it wirelessly to his phone. After another moment's inspection, he figured out how to activate its always-on flash. Then, making sure the camera was set to stream directly to Gray's cloud storage (via his phone's satellite service), he pointed the lens—and flashlight—into his own face... and began recording.

"My name is Grayson Gaynes," he said, voice hoarse and muffled by his balaclava. Blinking against the bright light, he pulled the knit mask below his chin and tried again. "My name is Grayson Gaynes, private investigator and retired NYPD homicide detective." He turned the device around and strapped it onto his forehead using the integrated headband. "I am investigating the derelict yacht *Bowhead Two*, site of the murder of David Aġviq Simmonds." Gray turned his head to get a good shot of the yacht's transom, which proudly displayed the boat's name and port of origin—*Bowhead II*, San Francisco, USA—painted in a rich goldleaf that glittered under the camera's bright flash. Filming in the dark like this, the little spotlight made it very clear what was in frame, which was good. Gray was not much of a cameraman.

"This visit is pursuant to my conversation with North Slope Borough Police Department detective Kyle Jameson this morning, January 9, 2024, at 8:18 a.m. local Alaska Standard Time, in which Detective Jameson indicated that this scene is released for my review... though the NSBPD declined to provide transport or accompany me. It is now..." He checked his phone. "... just after 5 p.m. of the same day, same time zone."

Gray got to work, unloading his supplies onto the yacht's low-lying swim deck, then ferrying them up a half-flight of steps to the raised aft deck. He looked around at the exposed lounge space, making sure to actually turn his head so the camera got it all: outdoor table and seating, a mini fridge, even a barbecue grill; off to one side, a narrow door hung open, exposing a small enclosure with a commode. Convenient. Then Gray turned his attention to the four wide sliding glass doors, currently closed but shattered, so that only jagged tooth-like shards clung to the frame around the outside.

Their edges were dark with frozen blood.

"Having reviewed crime scene photos and initial reports, I know that local police believe the problem bear made entry to the yacht via these glass doors," Gray narrated. He carefully grasped a door handle through one of his thick winter gloves, sliding the broken door out of the way and shining his light on the carpeted floor within. "Based on the pattern of broken glass, mostly *in*side the boat, I see no reason to disagree with this assessment. There is only a limited amount of blood, indicating flesh wounds only, not the fatal wounds suffered by the human victim in the cabin below deck. Plus, spectroscopy at the state police lab already confirmed samples taken here as being animal blood, polar bear specifically."

Stepping inside, boots crunching on broken glass, Gray continued his narrated exploration of the boat's middle deck. The sizable open kitchen or 'galley' to the left—port side—featuring all the normal kitchen appliances, including another mini fridge. The breakfast nook to the right, side by side with a *third* fridge for cooling wine, then a liquor cabinet, and what looked like a tall fuse box/server closet, though all the LEDs were dark. Forward of galley and nook was a lounge with roomy sofa seating for at least a dozen. And on all four sides of the immense open space were argon-insulated glass windows, intact aside from the broken sliding doors to stern. Despite that exposure behind him, it was remarkable how much warmer *and* quieter it was here, protected from the wind, which had picked up to a steady 25 mph through the afternoon. Gray checked the cheap digital thermometer clipped to his coverall zipper and smiled gratefully: no worse than -1° F.

Even abandoned and damaged as it was, the exaggerated luxury of this one deck was incredible: the redundancy of refrigerators; the cushioned outside sunbathing space both fore *and* aft, for a craft that spent half its time in the Arctic; the sheer amount of living space. The room Gray stood in now easily exceeded the square footage of the apartment he and Rose shared their first year of marriage, not even counting the sleeping quarters down below—and all of it for a single occupant. Gray wanted to poke fun at the opulence for the sake of the camera, but he held his tongue, opting for professionalism. The point of this video was to document exactly how he found things and what he touched, as much for his own future reference as possible use in court. It should also protect him from any accusations of contamination, though Jameson had little basis to make such a claim after clearly stating that law enforcement was done with the scene.

Climbing the stairs to the top deck flybridge, Gray found it to be another open space that dwarfed his newlywed nook. Even with hands enclosed in thick gloves, he had touched nothing below aside from the door handle; and he was careful to continue that pattern here, even noting it aloud for the camera. He pointed out the presence of more lounge seating up top, along with a huge work table strewn with maps. Here he finally removed his ski gloves, wincing as he snapped on a latex pair that did nothing to protect him from the cold. He flipped carefully through the oversized, unrolled papers, making sure to get a good shot of each for the camera before proceeding. They appeared to chart underwater topography and were heavily annotated in fine-tip permanent marker, the various dotted lines tracking the migration routes of specific whale pods. It was actually rather fascinating, but Gray decided it was unrelated to the murder and eventually forced himself to set the maps aside.

At the fore of this deck was the bridge itself, from which the yacht was steered. There was an actual steering wheel, like he might find on a car, but the surrounding 'dashboard' was a dizzying array of touchscreen displays and more traditional mechanical controls. How much of it was standard and how much custom, either to allow single-man operation or in pursuit of David's work as a marine biologist, Gray couldn't say. As below, the electronics here were all dark, and he wasn't about to start pushing buttons.

With a deep breath, hands clenched against the cold to come, Gray stepped out onto the exposed rear of the flybridge. "I'm not sure how well you can see it," Gray said for the camera, slowly panning his field of view left and right, then down, "but there's some sort of crane and winch assembly here, for raising and lowering this... um... lifeboat. Or actually, this is probably what Mr. Simmonds would use to go ashore. From what I understand, Utqiaġvik has no deepwater ports, so he would have to anchor the *Bowhead* a ways out, then launch this little craft." Little? Gray measured with his eyes, decided even this smaller motorboat was almost 15 feet in length—not significantly smaller than Dawn's own 20-foot cabin cruiser, which she considered a reasonable size. Shaking his head, Gray unsnapped and yanked back the stiff, snow-crusted tarp, gazing within to find the 'little' boat empty aside from some life jackets.

Remaining outside, Gray descended to the middle deck once more—using yet another staircase, not a ladder—and circled the craft. As spacious as it was inside, there was still another three feet of exposed decking all the way around the yacht's perimeter, along with a tale gunwale to protect from spray or any risk of falling overboard.

At the front of the ship once more—the bow, Gray reminded himself—something caught his eye and he knelt among the lounge seats, brushing away the half inch of loose snow. "Aha!" he said in mild victory. "I thought I saw something here. It's some sort of hatch, for underdeck storage." He grasped at the clasp mechanism with numb fingers, pulling it up and twisting to unbatten the small door, which he then flipped open. The space below was a couple feet deep and stuffed with more life vests. Gray picked through them quickly to ensure nothing was hidden, then began to close the hatch.

He hesitated. "What's this?" he mused, leaning forward and pointing with a latex-clad finger. "There appears to be a scuff mark along the side of this storage locker, the kind a rubber soled shoe might make. Except it's in an awkward, hard to reach place... and notice how the scuff is thickest and darkest where it meets the *bottom* of the locker?"

Curiosity piqued, Gray started pulling vests out of the space and flinging them aside. Then he felt carefully around the insides of the locker, which proved harder than expected with numb fingers, until... *there*. A finger-sized hole, invisible unless he pointed his camera headlamp right at it. Shoving one index finger in, Gray jiggled around until—with a snap of icy rime—the entire bottom of the locker came away in his hand. So he pulled *it* out and set it aside with the vests.

Revealing a much larger enclosure, complete with ladder. Along one side, he could now see that the scuff mark actually extended deeper into the boat.

"What have we here?" Excited, Gray shone his light and camera around the interior, then quickly descended the rungs. "It's not quite deep enough for me to stand fully—and would be even less so with the false cabinet floor installed, but... yes, this is still a sizable space hidden inside the bow of the ship." He bent, took a few steps, turned. "But is it actually meant to be secret, or just a convenient place to store stuff? If Mr. Simmonds *was* smuggling drugs, this would be a great place for it. Plenty of room, and likely to be completely overlooked on casual inspection by Coast Guard or whoever else." Gray's foot nudged something soft, and he snapped his head down to look. But it was just some plastic seat cushions from upstairs, three or four of them strewn about the fiberglass floor. "Or maybe this is just where he stored his lounge furniture pillows for the winter."

Sighing, Gray climbed the ladder back up and reset the quasi-secret compartment the way he'd found it. Then he re-entered the yacht proper, descending now to the lower deck—where it grew quieter, darker, and warmer still: 3° *above* zero. Still not enough to thaw out his fingers, though, so Gray got a couple of hand warmers from his pack and shook to activate them.

His camera light revealed a single narrow corridor running the length of the vessel, right down the middle. Cabin doors lined the sides, three on the left, just one on the right. Police tape wrapped the first door on the left side—the starboard side, since he was now facing aft—but Gray had already decided to leave the actual crime scene for last. The single door across the hall entered into an extensive master cabin suite that stretched along the entire port hull of the boat: a generous bedroom with king-sized bed led to a walk-in closet, which in turn accessed a long bathroom with double sinks and lots of vanity space, ending at commode and shower stalls. In each of these spaces, short-wide windows set at eye level offered a view across the sea, or would have if there'd been any light to see by.

Gray backtracked through the suite, narrating all the way, then explored the last two rooms on the other side: a guest cabin with small bathroom and four bunk beds, stacked two and two; and a combination pantry/laundry room, with full-size washer, dryer, and utility sink. (Again, the twenty-seven year old newlywed deep inside tried not to be jealous.) And at the very back of the ship, Gray found the engine room.

With a deep breath, he returned to the first door and pulled fabric booties over his shoes. Then, finally, he peeled away the police tape and stepped into David Simmonds' office.

There was blood *everywhere*, reminding Gray powerfully of the crime scene from the 'hellhound' murder years before. This was hardly surprising—multiple large-caliber slugs fired at close range into a human body tended to make an awful mess—but it was still horrific, even when reduced to gray tones. At least there was no smell, thanks to the cold.

What had been found of the body itself was now gone, of course, long since reunited with the remains from the bear's gullet. The autopsy had been completed, revealing nothing unexpected, and the body was bound for proper burial. The authorities had *not* marked the original location of each body part with chalk or tape, as that was largely a thing of the past; but thanks to the photos, Gray knew exactly where the man's lower torso and legs had been situated (partially eaten and dragged into one corner of the room) and where his dismembered right arm was recovered (shoved awkwardly under the desk). Even in Gray's memory, that sight was grisly.

Breathing carefully, he bent over each location in turn to examine how overlapping patterns of blood spatter had soaked into the carpet. Some part of him had expected to see secondary spray and streaks from when the bear began savaging the body, but of course the victim's blood had congealed and frozen long before the wildlife found it.

Standing, Gray panned his view—and the camera—across the office, noting other details:

The splintered door jamb, where the killer had kicked in the cabin door.

The wall hangings, including some expensive-looking original artwork as well as three expensively-framed diplomas (BS, MS, PhD) all mounted securely to the bulkheads.

The desk, built of highly-polished genuine wood and bolted to the floor, its drawers left open and empty after the police collected their contents into evidence—none of which had offered any new insight into what extracurricular activities the victim was involved in.

The desk chair, high-backed and clearly ergonomic, still lying where David knocked it over in his mad backpedal to escape fate.

And lastly, the three thumb-sized gouges in the wall behind desk and chair, where three .44 Magnum slugs—fired by Dawn's gun—had been cut from the gore-crusted bulkhead.

All of it exactly as photographed, aside from removal of David's remains. And much of it covered with the recognizable residue of fingerprint dust.

A residue that Gray now realized was lacking throughout the rest of the yacht. "Obviously, the CSI folks lifted lots of fingerprints in this room," he said for the camera's benefit. "But not anywhere outside of here, so far as I noticed. I for one am curious who else's prints we might find, aside from the victim and his accused murderer." He rummaged again in his pack. "Fortunately, I brought my own fingerprinting supplies—cornstarch and cocoa powder are both good options—as well as clear packing tape to lift any interesting prints. And of course there's this." He hefted a battery powered UV blacklight.

Working his way back through the rest of the yacht, Gray confirmed that he wasn't mistaken. The crime scene investigators had only dusted for prints in that one room. And because the prints they found fit their working theory, they'd never seen a need to return and dust elsewhere. But Gray was operating under a different theory.

So he started in David's master suite across the hall, switching back and forth between camera light and black light until he identified clear prints that could be lifted cleanly—as opposed to the useless mess of smeared, overlapping prints that typically adorned commonly used fixtures like door handles and faucet knobs. It was slow, painstaking work, but the P.I. lifted latent prints from a paperback novel on the bedside stand, two from the bedside itself, several partials from the bathroom mirror and shower stall, and one pristine full right handprint from the wall behind the commode. (Actually, experience had told him to look for that one first.) Having located a print with his black light, he would apply the 'dust' with one of the fine-bristled paint brushes he brought—cornstarch for dark surfaces and cocoa powder for light—then lift with tape, fold the tape against itself to preserve the print, label it with permanent marker, and seal it inside a separate snack-sized zipper baggie for good measure. Of course, most or all of the prints in David's suite likely belonged to David himself, but Gray didn't have a way of making that determination here in the field. He would have to lift *every* potentially meaningful print, then impose on Jameson or Abe to get them analyzed once he returned.

After the master suite, Gray examined the guest bed/bathroom again, then the pantry/laundry room, the engine room, and both of the open spaces on the decks above. Gray even examined the bow storage space for good measure, along with all the other storage lockers he discovered and the lifeboat too.

And what he found had staggering implications.

Because he didn't find *anything*. Not one solitary fingerprint, or even a mess of overlapping prints, aside from the ones in David's office and bedroom suite. Not on the washing machine or dryer. Not on the pantry shelves, which were suspiciously bare, considering a man lived here full time. Not on any of the three refrigerators or any of the cookware, or even on any of the helm controls.

It was, quite frankly, impossible... unless the scene had been tampered with before the cops even arrived. For that was the only reasonable explanation: someone had painstakingly wiped down every surface on this boat *except* the ones they *knew* bore only certain fingerprints—surfaces in rooms frequented only by David Simmonds.

That still didn't explain how *Dawn*'s fingerprints had appeared in these spaces too, when she swore she'd never been aboard. But it did prove that Dawn was not the person who tampered with the crime scene. For if Dawn had gone to all the trouble of cleaning the rest of this boat, then she certainly would have done the same for David's private bedroom, bathroom, and office—especially if she really had left her fingerprints on his desk after murdering him.

Gray felt an immense weight lift from his shoulders, a burden that had been steadily growing in the month since Dawn was arrested for murder. His intuition was not wrong. Dawn *was* innocent.

There was no longer any room for doubt in Gray's mind. Dawn Simmonds was being framed for the murder of her brother.

Gray woke with a start.

Heart racing, he stared into the utter darkness, trying to remember where he was, and why it was so damn *cold*. He could literally feel his breath misting before his face.

He gradually relaxed as it all came back to him. Having finished his investigation of the *Bowhead II*, he'd retrieved the rest of his gear from the yacht's aft deck, then returned here—to the guest bedroom with its four bunkbeds. After so long spent burning the candle at both ends, Gray had known (even before leaving U-Turn) that it would be one risk too many to embark on his return trip without at least a few hours of sleep. All by itself, the trip to the yacht had taken eight grueling hours. Add to that another four-plus hours of focused investigation, and it was 10 p.m. by the time he'd set up these temporary quarters. His need for rest had become quite desperate.

The first order of business had been cranking up Ephron's battery-operated space heater, which was good for an extra twenty degrees when positioned right next to him. Then Gray had wrapped himself in both a thick woolen blanket and a thin aluminum sheet designed to reflect most of his body heat back at him. So ensconced, he had bolted down a banana and a thermos of gloriously lukewarm chicken noodle soup before pulling out one of his precious Christmas gifts from Samuel's family: a box of fine chocolates. Feeling remarkably nostalgic for that day—barely two weeks past, but somehow vastly distant—Gray selected a toffee and a ganache heart before carefully resealing the gourmet treats that remained. And as he savored his selections, he remembered the games he played with Aurora and Luca, and felt gratitude toward Meredith for his new woolen socks (both pairs of which he was already wearing). At last, eyes drooping almost happily, Gray had collapsed to sleep on one of David Simmonds' guest bunks.

Now, bleary-eyed and head pounding, Gray registered that the LED on his space heater had gone out. He fumbled for his cell phone. It was... an hour after midnight, meaning the battery had lasted less than three hours, as expected. By the glow from his screen, he read 18° F off his zipper thermometer, meaning the cold was already fast returning—probably what had wakened him. So with a sigh, he dug in his pack for the other battery and plugged it in before stumbling into the small bathroom (or 'head' as it was called on a boat) to relieve himself.

At this point, Gray had no concerns about leaving his own DNA or fluids behind, considering both he and law enforcement had completed their crime scene investigation—*and* since this cabin had been contaminated long before that anyway, wiped clean by the real killer. Still, Gray refilled his soup thermos instead of the commode, which had ruptured months ago when the water in the bowl froze. Decency dictated that Gray's only other option was going topside and peeing over the gunwale, and that simply *wasn't* an option—not when the temp outside was still well below zero. Some parts of the body just weren't worth risking to instant frostbite.

Afterwards, he settled back onto his borrowed bunk and tried to get comfortable. He still wanted a couple more hours of shuteye before setting out.

Unfortunately, with a few hours already under his belt, his mind began churning once more, and further sleep proved elusive. Someone had gone to a lot of trouble to frame Dawn Simmonds for the murder of her brother. But who, and just as importantly, why? And if that person wanted Dawn to take the fall, why leave matters in such a state that the body might never be discovered? What if that bear had never found David's corpse, and what if it hadn't been shot hassling a child, and what if David's remains hadn't been identified in its belly? What if the *Bowhead* had lost its anchor and got pulled out to sea, or else was damaged by the ice and sank? In any of those events, it was entirely possible David's death would never be discovered. Considering his work and travel patterns, it might be years before he was even reported missing, and a minimum of seven more years before he was presumed dead from a legal standpoint.

And short of *that*, the video log implicating Dawn in his murder never would have been found. So why go to so much trouble fabricating further evidence against her, when there was a good chance none of it would be discovered for a decade or more?

Because the entire frame job was just a contingency plan, Gray realized. Not the video log, in which the victim cried out his killer's name—letting *that* critical piece of evidence get reported and stored in the cloud where it couldn't be doctored was obviously a mistake on the killer's part. The coincidence that David's sister was named Dawn must have been what led the real killer to choose her as the most plausible suspect for the frame. But the frame job itself was all a contingency, all of that false evidence carefully crafted and planted *just in case* David's last video log was ever discovered, be it tomorrow or ten years from now. And *that* was more than a little chilling to Gray, even on top of how cold he already was. It suggested that the killer was a very careful individual, willing to go to great trouble and expense to cover himself (or herself?) in the event of an outcome that wasn't even guaranteed.

It also suggested something further, Gray realized. If that was the kind of person who killed David Simmonds, they were clearly quite capable of killing him in a way that left *no* risk of evidence pointing back at themselves. Instead, they had killed David with the ideal ammunition to facilitate ballistics identification, *and* David had found the time to record exactly seventy-six seconds of video that might have included even more damning testimony, had he chosen his words differently.

This murder really wasn't premeditated. It was a knee-jerk reaction to something unanticipated.

But what? What in the world had David been doing out here, beyond studying the mating and migration patterns of whales? If he was truly part of some drug trafficking operation, had it been unwitting? Was *that* what took him by surprise on the day of his death? Gray wished yet again that he could comb through the victim's laptop instead of just his cloud storage, but the computer had not been found at the scene. The killer had apparently absconded with it in the fateful minutes after the laptop's little webcam recorded its owner's murder.

Gray's headache was now even worse than before. Sighing, he found some ibuprofen in his bag and swallowed the max dosage, then turned over, determined to fall asleep. But he wasn't used to sleeping without a pillow, and this mattress was especially lumpy.

No, it wasn't lumpy, Gray realized. He was having a princess-and-the-pea moment. There was something *under* the mattress, and he'd probably just been too tired to realize it earlier. Reaching beneath the bedding, he fished around until he found the offending item, then turned on his flashlight again.

It was a little stuffed animal, barely larger than his hand—a sort of koala teddy bear with big ears and big eyes, its fur dark except on face and chest. Now *that* was an odd thing to find in a floating bachelor pad.

And how had they missed this? Not just Gray himself, but the police and even the killer? Probably very easily, he decided. The cops had been focused next door, and Gray already knew they hadn't given the rest of the ship as much attention as they should. And for his own part, well, Gray was just one man.

He carefully placed the little doll in a gallon-sized zipper bag and tucked it in his pack with the fingerprint evidence, then restored his winter gloves and flopped back on the mattress. The boat was rocking gently in the tide, and with that motion lulling him, Gray finally started drifting back to sleep.

Wait. The boat was rocking?

He shot up to a sitting position once more, eyes wide, ears straining. Because the boat *shouldn't* be rocking. It was stuck fast in the ice. In all the hours he spent searching the yacht before finally settling down, he'd never felt any of the sway he normally associated with being out to sea. So why now?

Then he heard it. A strange... snuffling... that raised the hair on the back of Gray's neck. But it was so faint and indistinct, and the ensuing silence so lengthy, that he began to think he'd imagined it.

The silence was shattered by an explosive snort, the kind that can only be generated by a creature with a 100-liter lung capacity.

Gray's lips parted, and out slipped the most vile compound curse he knew. Then he jumped to his feet and ran to the door, peeking out. The hall was clear. Turning, he shut off the space heater, then shouldered just one pack—the one containing his evidence baggies, emergency beacon, and the rest of his food. Gray's phone was already in his right chest pocket, and fortunately, he had gone to sleep fully clothed and shod, more to stay warm than out of a sense of preparedness.

He fled the room, moving as quickly and quietly as he could, reaching the front of the ship in moments and creeping up the bow stairs on all fours. Slowing as he reached the top, Gray saw the sofas first, the indoor lounge area on the middle deck. Raising his head ever so carefully, he swiveled to look aft, towards the kitchen galley.

And there it was. *Inside* the yacht between the galley and the breakfast nook, no more than fifteen feet from where Gray now trembled. Standing upright on back legs and still unable to reach its full height under the 8-foot ceiling, the massive creature's head and shoulders hunched as its snout undulated, tasting the air.

A polar bear. *Another* magnificent *polar bear.* A sight that had always invoked hush and reverence in Gray before now... and today inspired terror.

The beast snorted again, its head snapping to look straight at Gray as it crashed back onto all fours. Gray was already moving, diving up the stairs and throwing open one of the forward sliding doors. He tripped through, resisting the urge to look back but *feeling* as the bear collided with the other glass panel. It slowed the beast, but only slightly. The hatch to David Simmonds' special compartment lay before Gray's face—closed, of course, for Gray just *had* to leave it how he found it—so he kept going, stumbling toward the pointy front of the ship. He could smell the bear's fetid breath as it huffed angrily, but he didn't look back, instead throwing himself over the three-foot rail.

Gray fell for a short eternity, most of a second, before *cracking* onto the snow-swept ice seven feet below. He howled in pain. It wasn't the ice that had broken, but his arm. Good thing he hadn't landed on his feet.

No time to lick his wounds. Gray stumbled up, off-balance due to the pack still strapped over both shoulders. Then he was running.

The snowmobile took a much longer eternity to start. He lost track of how many times he jerked the pull cord, the motion awkward with his non-dominant hand. Simultaneously, he was slipping the safety tether over his broken arm and ignoring the pain as he turned the ignition key and choke lever back and forth, in every possible combination of positions, unable to remember how it went and unable to see in the dark. His brain was so fuzzy! Meanwhile, beside him, the boat rocked violently as the thousand-pound bear reacquired Gray's scent and came charging back through the rear of the yacht towards him.

Damn polar bears and their supernatural sense of smell. Double-damn polar bears and their if-it-moves-it's-food mentality. Damn *Gray* for not bringing a gun, and to hell with being gun-shy after the Catskills—and to *triple*-hell with his employment contract, which explicitly forbad oil field workers from carrying firearms. This situation was *exactly* why every sane person in the North Slope carried a large caliber handgun at all times. Not that Ephron would have loaned him his Smith & Wesson 29, since *he* needed it, but damn Gray for not even *asking*.

Gray jerked the cord again and again, cursing with every pull—and at last, the engine caught, roaring victoriously. The bear roared back, and Gray was sure he felt spittle on his face.

He leapt aboard and opened up the throttle. The snow machine leapt forward a mere three feet before fishtailing and colliding with the yacht, throwing Gray clear. Head striking hard against the transom, the P.I. rolled and came up, seeing stars. What—

The rope. Gray had tied the snowmobile to one of the *Bowhead*'s mooring cleats when he first arrived. "You moron, *why?!*" he wailed. It's not like the snowmobile was going to float away!

Staggering to his feet, Gray almost lost his head to the swipe of a gigantic paw. There was the bear, leaning double over the stern railing, *reaching* for him. Gray tripped backwards, mouth gone dry, all cursed out.

And suddenly, he realized, all was silence aside from the bear's frustration. The snowmobile's ignition had cut when Gray was thrown, thanks to the safety tether—and just as well, or the thing might still be accelerating into the hull of the yacht. Biting off one glove, Gray dug into a coverall pocket to grab his multitool, extending the serrated blade. Two inches long, it was useless against the bear, but against that rope...

Mercifully, the enraged bear couldn't seem to remember how it had gotten aboard the yacht, instead racing back and forth along the stern rail as Gray freed and restarted the snowmobile. The P.I. put the machine through a quick turn and then throttled away from the yacht a second time, risking a look back only when he was safely out of reach.

The bear had climbed atop the stern rail. Teetering there, it looked down at the ice, then raised its eyes to meet Gray's.

And jumped.

Gray was maybe fifty feet from the boat when the bear hit the ice. Bear and ice moaned as one, and Gray's whole world tilted backwards. The snow machine shot out from under him, disappearing over a sudden rise, and then Gray was sliding back the other way. He rolled, trying to sit up, pointing his feet in the direction he was moving.

The bear was gone, but there was now an open pool of black water at the rear of the boat—exactly where Gray was about to splash down. He got his feet under him and jumped at the last possible moment.

He almost made it, his naked non-dominant hand—which he hadn't had time to re-glove—grabbing desperately at the mooring cleat before sliding down the frayed length of his own rope until he finally got a grip.

Gray's bottom half went in the drink.

He gasped, head thrown back in voiceless agony. Two years of experience as a roustabout, sometimes working for hours at a time in -50° conditions, and yet *nothing* could have prepared him for the anguish of this moment. For in that instant, it felt like every remaining ounce of warmth fled him, as if his soul itself was being sucked out in one last prolonged exhale.

Then Gray inhaled violently and *screamed.*

Pulling, *heaving* against rope and cleat, he got his legs back out of the water. It felt a colossal task; not only had the cold robbed him of his strength, but the water seeping into his many layers had doubled his weight as well. Yet he did it, pulling himself onto the swim deck and sobbing, his relief quickly turning to defeat as he realized his likely fate. He was now soaked to the waist and lay exposed to subzero temps, which could only mean that—

The polar bear's head popped out of the inky black depths, caught sight of him, and roared yet again. Unlike Gray, this fellow was in his element and angrier than ever.

Gray found one last reservoir of strength and rolled the other direction. Colliding with a stair step, he heaved himself up the half-flight of stairs to the yacht's aft deck on arm strength alone; he couldn't even feel his body beneath the waist, much less put it to use. Reaching the top, he army-crawled along the starboard gunwale, sobbing, tears and snot frozen before reaching his chin. Behind him, he heard the bear's claws scrabbling for purchase against the transom. If not for the broken ice, the bear having to heave its own thousand-pound bulk from the water, it would already be aboard—and Gray would already be dead.

Gray's increasingly befuddled sense of self-preservation screamed at him to go below deck, to the bunk room with the space heater and blankets. But no, if the last bear had squeezed itself into David's office, this one could reach Gray there too. He *knew* that. It was why he'd fled, and—

He was at the bow of the ship now, and there was the hatch. The smuggling compartment.

The fingers of Gray's exposed left hand were no longer responding, so he unbattened the hatch clumsily with the hand of his broken arm, then lifted the false bottom free—another sob ripping from his throat at the pain shooting up that arm. He tried to slide sidewise, dropping his legs into the hole to feel for the ladder, but there *was* no feeling below the waist. His pants leg caught and he tumbled in face-first, landing hard on his shoulder.

For the longest time, he just lay that way, half upside-down, breath heaving. "Ow," he said simply, then erupted in hoarse, hysterical laughter that quickly gave way to wracking coughs.

Then the boat began rocking again.

Gray finished collapsing, maneuvering himself awkwardly in the tight confines, then reaching for the ladder rungs with his one 'good' hand. He straightened up, wedging his screaming shoulders into the corner of the space so he wouldn't collapse again on noodle-like legs, repeating the process over and over, inch by inch, until he could reach the open hatch overhead.

Another roar, fetid breath.

Gray slammed the hatch closed above him, granting himself the thinnest veneer of protection from winter, wind, and wildlife, before collapsing again in total darkness. He groped, found a few lounge cushions, and made himself as comfortable as possible. Then he fumbled the emergency beacon out of his bag and managed to activate it before tossing the little device aside. In theory, that should be enough for Search & Rescue to find him.

But what about the bear? What if it hunkered down inside the yacht, and they didn't see it before sending personnel down a ladder to rescue Gray? He should really *call* someone—Jameson?—to make them aware.

Gray checked his phone. It showed battery at 8%, the time only 1:30 a.m. So many eternities had elapsed in the last half hour. Wait, what had he been trying to do just now? And why was his screen so dim and blurry? Where was the...

Oh. Right. Jameson. Gray managed to connect a call but got the man's voicemail, so he hung up. No, that was wrong... he was operating on autopilot. He had something he needed to communicate, even if that meant leaving a message. Everything was just... so... fuzzy... right now. Blinking forcefully, he focused on his phone screen and jabbed one numb finger to redial. Too rough. The phone slipped through his fingers, clattering out of sight. Ever so faintly in the darkness, he heard the detective's voicemail prompt, so Gray spoke as loudly as possible and hoped his words carried:

"Uh... Detective Jameson? Hi... hello... um." He thought really hard. "This is Grayson Gaynes, NYPD detect—no. No, just... Grayson Gaynes. I need... some assistance," he slurred. "I'm onboard the *Bowhead*, and... uh... I made a new friend."

Gray was still talking when he finally succumbed to unconsciousness.

Thursday to Saturday, January 11 - 13th
Utqiaġvik

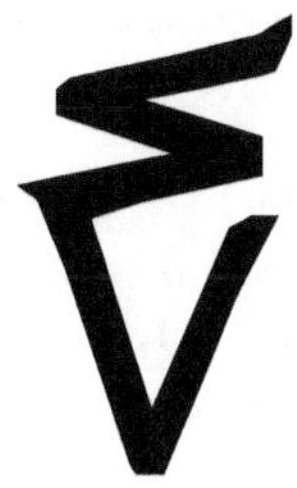

Gray woke disoriented for the second time in a row. Reaching fuzzily for his cell phone on a bedside table, he checked the time and then noticed the date, cursing. He'd lost a whole day—actually more like 36 hours since he'd gone toe-to-toe with that monster of a polar bear. Now he was in a hospital bed, in a hospital room, IVs pushing fluids into his left arm, his right arm in a cast. And... one foot was handcuffed to the bed rail.

He stared stupidly at the cuffs for a long moment until laughter drew his attention.

An Iñupiaq woman had appeared in the doorway, vending machine coffee cup in one hand, laptop tucked under her other arm. For a hopeful moment, he thought it was Dawn, already exonerated and released—but no. "Esther?" he realized, his voice a barely decipherable rasp.

Esther frowned in obvious disappointment. "With your face thing, I thought I'd have you guessing a little longer than *that*." She cocked her head. "You recognized my tunniit—um, my tattoos?"

Gray nodded, coughing to get his voice back. "They're as unique to me as your face would be to everyone else."

She lit up at this. Everyone liked the reminder that they were one-of-a-kind. Setting down her coffee, she made a quick phone call. "He's awake!" she reported before hanging up. Then to Gray: "Sorry to laugh, but the look on *your* face when I walked in... you didn't expect to find yourself handcuffed, or I guess footcuffed?"

"No, not really."

"Don't worry. Detective Jameson is pissed, talking about crime scene contamination and obstruction of justice, but he's decided not to charge you. He just didn't want you wandering off."

Gray snorted at the suggestion he'd acted illegally, but decided against arguing the point. Talking hurt too much. "Am I gonna make it?" he asked instead, only half joking. He could manage short, simple sentences without as much discomfort.

"Probably," Esther said brightly. "But you're going to be a while recovering. Let's see if I can remember all the things you did to yourself." Leaning over, she tapped his plaster cast. "Broke your right arm. Your scapula too—I think that's your shoulder blade?" She took his left hand in hers, flipping it over. "Serious abrasions, maybe rope burns, on this hand, plus frostbite. You almost lost your pinky, and jury's still out on a few of your toes. You were suffering severe hypothermia and exposure when they found you, core temperature super low." She thought for a moment. "Multiple other contusions and fractures, I think; can't remember where. Oh! And you're concussed."

"I feel concussed," Gray admitted.

"You *look* concussed," she agreed with a laugh. "You sure that didn't happen *before* you undertook this stupid-ass stunt? Even my people don't go skinny dipping this time of year."

He snorted, paused. "And Dawn?" he asked quietly.

Esther shrugged. "No change. Still in jail."

"But this new evidence, my findings, it changes everything," Gray said, only realizing after he said it how the words mirrored David's own statement just moments before his murder. "You reviewed my footage from the boat, yes?"

"We did. And... maybe," she allowed. "I'll let Samuel answer that."

The big lawyer arrived at the hospital less than fifteen minutes later, which was good, since Esther refused to say more and Gray's impatience was about to get the better of him.

"That was smart," Samuel said, "sharing your cloud storage with me before you even left U-Turn—

especially since nothing else you did was terribly intelligent."

"You watched it all?"

"Every minute."

"So you agree," Gray said excitedly, struggling to sit up straighter in his bed. "The fact that every other cabin in the *Bowhead II* was wiped clean proves that Dawn's not the killer."

Samuel slowly nodded. "I agree that Dawn wouldn't have cleaned the rest of the boat but forgotten the room where she committed a murder."

Gray frowned. "You think the killer and the cleaner are two different people?"

"It's certainly one possibility the prosecution might argue, though they hardly need to."

"But—" Gray began to object.

"Look, you've convinced *me*," Samuel said hurriedly, hands up in a calming gesture. "I'm no longer advising Dawn to take a plea deal. We're going to fight this in court."

"But the cops? They haven't dropped the charges?" Gray asked, incredulous.

"Entirely aside from the fact that Jameson and the DA's office have charged Dawn with more than just murder, no. They haven't dropped any of the charges."

Gray slammed one fist onto the mattress in frustration. "Why the hell not?"

"Because your new findings *don't* actually prove anything. It may not make sense why Dawn would clean the rest of the boat and not the office, but that doesn't mean she didn't commit the murder. With your experience, you of all people know that stupidity, insanity, even simple mistakes cause people to do all sorts of things that don't make sense. Meanwhile, the cops can't ignore the mountain of other facts standing against her." He hesitated, giving Gray an apologetic smile. "Even I think the authorities are duty-bound to carry the case to trial. It's a *jury's* job to weigh all that evidence against whether the narrative makes sense. At this point, only a jury should decide that Dawn is innocent."

"But we *are* fighting this," Esther reiterated, seeing how Gray had deflated. "Not taking a plea. Because this whole thing smells wrong. It's just too bad Dawn has to rot in jail for months awaiting a court date."

Samuel nodded firmly, placing a big hand on Gray's uninjured shoulder and looking him in the eye. "Gray. You did good. I know this wasn't the outcome you hoped for, but it's not nothing." He barked a disbelieving laugh. "Taking a snow machine thirty miles onto the ice and trading blows with a bear was beyond asinine, but the fact that you would take that risk... it means the world to Dawn. It gave her *hope*. She says thank you. We all do."

Gray nodded, weariness settling over him like a blanket.

"Though you probably owe her friend Ephron a new snow machine," Esther added helpfully.

Gray barked a laugh, though it hurt in more ways than one. Ephron had likely deposited his $8,000 check already, and Gray only hoped he didn't owe the man even more.

"Now get some rest," Samuel concluded, standing. "You need to heal up. I think the docs want to keep you here for a few days, so don't try to leave. I'm not sure how much more stupid you can survive."

"No worries," Gray said, wiggling his foot in its manacle. "I'm apparently not going anywhere."

The lawyer snorted. "Someone from the NSBPD should be by later today about that, since they've decided not to press charges."

Gray rolled his eyes at that. "But what am I supposed to do?" he asked. "Tied to this bed or not, I can't do *nothing* for a few days. You know me better than that by now."

"We sure do," Esther said with a grin, handing Gray the laptop. "We've been working so much overtime lately, Samuel gave me tomorrow off, so you can borrow my computer for the weekend. Stream some black and white movies or something."

It was a kind gesture, considering Gray had left his own laptop at Ephron's with the bulk of his other belongings, expecting to be back in less than 24 hours. "I'm glad you're getting a day off. You deserve it, but—" Gray shook his head. "*I* can't stop working the case. Not now, not after everything."

"Then don't," Esther told him with a twinkle in her eye. "All the case files are on that machine too."

"But stay *here*," Samuel pressed. "I want your promise, Gray."

Gray sighed. Beyond his desire to keep working this case, he really needed to get back to his actual job too. He'd only planned on skipping a single shift with this 'stunt', but he was now halfway through his *third* missed shift. Still, he nodded. "I promise, Samuel. I'll stay here until the docs release me." It wasn't like he'd be able to do much on the drill floor with just one arm anyway. "And thanks for trusting me with your computer, Esther."

They said their goodbyes. And despite everything he'd just said about needing to work, Gray's exhaustion soon overtook him again. He slept several more hours, only waking when Detective Jameson dropped by that evening to give him a stern talking-to, complete with a lot of name-calling. And while the cop did remove the 'footcuffs' before the end, he also promised Gray an itemized invoice for the chopper rescue—which would *not* be cheap. Between that, the inevitable hospital bills, and Ephron's snowmobile, this episode was going to wipe out Gray's savings.

"At least tell me I get a polar bear pelt out of this," Gray joked darkly.

"What, you think we killed that bear, just to rescue your sorry butt?" Jameson scoffed. "Hardly. We just hovered and yelled at it over the megaphone until it ran away."

"Did you recover my pack?" Gray asked, more seriously. "The one with the physical evidence?"

Jameson nodded. "We already analyzed the new fingerprints. All belonging to David Simmonds."

"And the stuffed animal? That little doll?"

At this, Jameson only shrugged. "I can't see how it's meaningful to the case, but I agree it seems out of place. So we'll keep it in the evidence locker with everything else from the boat."

Gray sighed, but it was no less than he'd expected. "At least send me some pictures, please?"

Jameson agreed, though he flatly refused to discuss the contamination that had obviously occurred before authorities even found the boat. Whatever it might mean—the fact that someone had cleaned the rest of the yacht aside from David's office and master suite—this case was going to trial.

Gray had a hard time swallowing solid food that night, preferring instead several cups of Jello. He even started an old movie, though with his worries about Dawn, he couldn't stomach a courtroom drama. Bypassing *12 Angry Men* and *To Kill a Mockingbird*, Gray settled on *Casablanca* instead.

And when the nurse woke him Friday morning, coming by on her 8 a.m. rounds, Gray was ready to get to work.

He started with the stuffed animal, the photos of which Jameson had just texted him. Gray inspected each of the dozen digital snapshots, which included a ruler for size comparison and employed better lighting than that dim bunk room on the *Bowhead II*. The toy was roughly eight inches tall, and Gray could now see just how tattered it was. That wasn't from exposure. It had the look of a child's favorite possession worn out by years of handling, and had even been doodled on in places, apparently with ink pen.

Thoughtful, Gray selected one of the photos and performed an online search using image recognition. The results were unambiguous. This little fellow was known as Чебурашка—Cheburashka—and he was a cartoon character from Soviet-era Russia. It was impossible to know how old this particular avatar was, however, for toymakers had been manufacturing plush toys in its likeness for decades, long after the fall of the Iron Curtain. Cheburashka dolls were even available at major retailers in the U.S. now. But, interesting as all that was, Gray simply couldn't see how the stuffed animal helped him solve this murder.

Gray opened the directory marked 'Simmonds' on Esther's laptop, digging once more into the mountain of evidence against Dawn. Finally somewhat rested (having slept more than 40 of the last

72 hours), Gray felt his brain might actually be capable of thinking analytically again. That was good, because he needed to identify what everyone had missed so far, the linchpin detail that—when pulled out into the light—would cause the entire case against Dawn to fall apart. Gray needed to prove not merely that Dawn *could* have been framed, but that she actually was.

The fact was, most of the individual items of evidence against her could be faked. No one would dispute that under oath, not even Jameson. Sure, David Simmonds' blood was in the tread of Dawn's work boots, but someone else could have been wearing her boots during the murder or even collected samples of his blood to apply to the tread after the fact. And the NSBPD couldn't prove the murder weapon had belonged to Dawn at the time of the murder, only that it was holstered on her hip when she was arrested three months later. As for DNA, hair and fibers could've easily been collected at her house and planted at the scene, and while that sort of contamination was more difficult to accomplish with latent fingerprints, it wasn't impossible. And lastly, as Gray had already established ad nauseum, the Dawn or Don whom David mentioned in his last-ever video log could literally apply to dozens of people.

The problem was, while most of the evidence against Dawn *could* be faked, it just seemed so implausible for *all* of it to be. And that overwhelming implausibility was exactly what made this frame-job so foolproof. Especially when you layered the fabricated evidence atop those facts that *couldn't* be faked:

The timeline, and the GPS data from Dawn's cabin cruiser.

Dawn had been at those coordinates in the Beaufort Sea (70°52'30.0"N 151°01'45.7"W) between 11:20 a.m. and 12:15 p.m. on September 13, according to timestamp and location data logged from a Starlink satellite—a fact that even Dawn attested. David had been murdered at 11:43 a.m. the same day, according to his video log, onboard a yacht that even now remained anchored at the same coordinates. The murder happened smack dab in the middle of the time the accused murderer spent at that rendezvous, no matter how strenuously she claimed that the other boat never appeared. And supposedly, none of this data could be faked.

Assuming Dawn's innocence, it seemed as obvious as ever what must have happened: David's boat had been *somewhere else* when the murder occurred, then moved to the rendezvous coordinates sometime after Dawn left. The real murderer had planted DNA and fingerprint evidence on the yacht, then planted drugs, money, and blood at Dawn's house and boat, *and* traded firearms with the young Iñupiaq woman at some point without her ever realizing—not to mention accessing her phone long enough to delete her text exchange with David, just to make her look even guiltier. As implausible as all that sounded, there were simply no other possibilities once you removed the impossibilities.

Unfortunately, only Gray and his friends were willing to assume Dawn's innocence, and the resulting narrative was *awfully* implausible.

And also, Gray realized suddenly, it broke his profile of the real killer. Lying in his borrowed bunk aboard the *Bowhead*, Gray had decided that David's murder could not have been premeditated. Now, he realized it must have been. For how else could the killer have known he needed to entice Dawn to those coordinates at that particular time?

Setting aside his borrowed computer, Gray thumbed through his phone until he found his text exchange with Samuel, which included screenshots of Dawn's text exchange with David on September 13. David's very first message struck Gray once more, as it had every time he read it:

> *Nayaaluk, I want to clear the air. Apologize in preson for everything. Before I sail south for the witner. Meet me tomorrow?*

It wasn't the typos that bothered Gray. He would probably find it more suspicious if the spelling and grammar were perfect. No, it was that very first word—*nayaaluk.* Samuel had said it meant 'little sister.'

But wait. Hadn't Dawn told him *David* was the younger sibling?

Gray called Samuel and posed the question. "*I noticed that at some point too*," the other man said. "*But Dawn assured me she was the older child.*"

"And David calling her 'little sister' didn't make her suspicious?" Gray asked skeptically. "Like maybe that wasn't really her brother texting?"

"*Not at all—not at the time. People say all sorts of goofy or ironic things when they're trying to be funny*," Samuel pointed out. "*Plus, you have to understand, lots of our people—especially the youth, especially someone like David—don't actually speak Iñupiaq. Dawn did notice the slip, but she assumed he was being playful or contrite. Besides, he* was *much taller than her. Apparently he liked to lord that over her when they were teens.*"

"What do you mean, contrite?"

"*Oh, like maybe David was making a concerted effort to show respect for the culture he had dishonored for so long. That same text did say he wanted to clear the air, after all.*"

"And now that Dawn knows someone is framing her? Does she still think it was David she was texting that day?"

"*Even now, she's just not sure.*" Samuel hesitated. "*What do* you *think?*"

"I'm leaning towards someone else. The real murderer, setting her up to take the fall."

But again, if the real killer had sent Dawn those texts before murdering David—somehow spoofing the messages to make them seem like they were coming from David's phone—that again meant the murder was premeditated. And if that was the case, why or how had this obviously careful, methodical killer allowed his victim a chance to record a 'deathbed' video? David could easily have spoken his killer's full name, and this entire investigation would have gone quite differently.

Hanging up with Samuel, Gray sagged back into his raised hospital bed. He was still missing something critical; he just had no idea what. So, with literally nothing else to do, he started going through David's video logs yet again—working his way backwards from the murder all the way to the beginning of the summer season, when David first returned to the Beaufort Sea. For hours on end, Gray watched as David documented his whale research in laborious detail, a new log entry every few days, often consisting of more than an hour of scientific minutia that sailed right over the P.I.'s head. But still he watched, and more than anything, he *listened.* He listened for even the vaguest reference to the drug smuggling operation the victim was supposedly involved in. He listened for any detail regarding the mysterious institute that supposedly underwrote the victim's research. Gray listened for *any* odd word that might be construed to cast the facts of the case in a new light, staring at that screen and straining his ears until he felt his eyes and ears alike were bleeding. Still, David Simmonds said nothing helpful.

And yet sometime Saturday night, Gray noticed something else—something everyone had easily missed before: Two of the video log entries from back in May overlapped.

It was subtle. Both entries were right at an hour long, and they only overlapped by ten minutes. But during those ten minutes, Gray had found apparent videographic evidence of David Simmonds discussing two entirely different topics at the same moment in time. An impossibility.

Which meant the video timestamps *could* be inaccurate. Maybe not doctored in this case (because why would the May logs have any bearing on the murder?), but certainly corrupt—even though the cloud service tech said he had verified the timestamps and would testify to their accuracy. Obviously he was wrong, but how? And how to prove it in a way that invalidated the entire case against Dawn, rather than merely introducing more doubt?

Gray thought back to the hellhound case he had worked all those years ago, and the way his entire timeline for the murder had been based on security card access logs. Gray had questioned the accuracy of the log timestamps in that case too, but hadn't had the technical acumen to uncover the truth for himself. He had needed to call in an expert.

Today, he found himself in the same situation, so he made the same call again.

Pulling out his phone, Gray dialed the number for his favorite resident geek.

"*Gray!*" cried the delighted voice of Bobbi Falmer. "*How the heck are you?*"

"I'm good, Bobbi. Thanks for taking my call." In point of fact, she had ignored his first call, seeing only an unknown number from Alaska on her caller ID. But then he'd texted her, telling her who it was, and she had instantly phoned him back. "I wasn't sure you would want to hear from me, after the way things ended," Gray added hesitantly.

"*Of course I would,*" she said brightly. "*I have the utmost respect for you, Double-G. Only a little less now than before all that Mad Batter business went down, but still lots more than I have for most of these clowns.*" By which she probably meant the other detectives in the NYPD homicide bullpen where she worked as a data forensics analyst.

Gray lifted an eyebrow at her live-wire energy. "Have you been pulling all-nighters hopped up on energy drinks again?"

"*Well, it* is *two in the morning on a Sunday, and I* am *up, so what do you think?*" she bubbled back with entirely too much vitality.

Gray winced. "Sorry, Bobbi, the time difference. It's only..." He checked. "Wow, it's already 10 p.m. here. Sorry," he repeated lamely.

"*Like I say, I'm already up. So yeah. What's up with you?*"

"Well, I'm calling to ask a favor," he began.

There was a long pause, and when Bobbi spoke again, she was noticeably less excited. "*Of course you are. Not just calling to say hi, catch up. I haven't heard a peep from you in almost* eight years. *No idea what you're doing with your life, where you're living, even if you're still alive. But no small talk. Just straight to the favor.*"

Now Gray truly felt awful. "I'm sorry, Bobbi. You're entirely right. And... I do want to catch up, hear how you've been. But this favor—"

"*I'm not doing anything illegal for you, Gray. And if you ask me to, my respect won't be so utmost anymore.*"

"No, no, nothing like that," he hurried to say. "I'm just..." He sighed. "I'm working as a P.I., trying to clear a woman who's been accused of murder."

"*Did she do it?*"

"What? No, I'm pretty confident she didn't. I wouldn't be trying to clear her name if I thought she was guilty."

"*Well, that's good. But the cops think she offed someone?*"

Gray leapt on this. "Oh yes. So if you help me clear her name, you'd be sticking it to the man." This was something of a running gag with Bobbi. Despite the fact that she worked for 'the man' herself, and really was a rule-follower at heart, she had long cultivated the persona of an anarchist hacker resigned to using her skills for evil just to make ends meet. Façade or not, however, the woman truly did have a soft spot for anyone the justice system had failed.

Indeed, the geek's mood seemed marginally improved when she responded. "*Well, okay then.*" Long pause. "*Is she cute?*"

Gray blinked at the non sequitur. "Who, Dawn?"

"*Is Dawn the chick you're trying to exonerate? Then yes, Dawn. Is she* cute*?*" Bobbi demanded again, suddenly playful.

"Um, yeah, I guess."

"*And single?*"

"Uh... yes."

"*Then what's the problem?*"

"The problem? Bobbi, I'm trying to get her out of jail. The last thing I'm thinking about right now is romance."

Gray's friend blew an audible raspberry across the line. "*Pffft. That's not what I mean, G-man. I'm asking the problem* with your case. *What is it you need my help with?*"

"Oh." And Gray felt very stupid. But he began to explain. "I have these video log entries. Tons of them. Same person in each. But two of the videos overlap—their timestamps do, I mean—so that tells me the data must've been corrupted or doctored, right?"

"*Maybe. Can you send me the files?*" And she walked him through uploading them to a team collaboration website, which of course took forever, since he decided to upload *all* of this year's videos. While they waited, Bobbi peppered him with questions about the files' origin and chain of custody. When Gray told her which cloud service had been used, she "*hmmed*" thoughtfully.

"What?" Gray asked.

"*I assume your local PD got a warrant to request these files direct from the cloud service? That company wouldn't have given them out otherwise.*"

"That's correct."

"*And their people confirmed the upload timestamps match the video timestamps?*"

"Yeah. Said they would testify and everything."

"*Then you can trust the timestamps. Those folks are legit, I assure you.*"

"Then how do you explain the overlap?" Gray pressed. "The victim couldn't have recorded two different videos of himself at the same time. It's impossible."

Bobbi chuckled. "*I have a thought, but give me a second to check now that I've got most of the videos downloaded. Let's see... which ones are overlapping?*"

"The two on May 21," he told her.

There was about a minute of relative silence over the line, punctuated only by mouse clicks and keyboard clacks. Then:

"*Yep, sure enough,*" Bobbi said. "*There's no reason to think these files have been doctored, corrupted, or modified in any way. Their timestamps don't actually overlap.*"

"Bobbi, I can *see* that they do. The first one ends at 4:33 p.m., while the next one begins nine minutes earlier, at 4:24 p.m. on the same date."

"*Yeah, but in two different time zones, man.*"

Gray was thunderstruck. "But... all of mainland Alaska is on the same time zone, and David Simmonds spent the entire summer just north of Alaska in the Beaufort Sea," he said, even though he was already questioning these facts all over again.

"*If you say so.*"

Gray's eyes narrowed. "Wait, how can you tell the time zone from these videos anyway? What are you seeing that I'm not?"

"*Do you want me to show you on these May 21 videos, or is there a different video that's more important to the case?*"

“September 13,” Gray said promptly. “The very last log entry. It... fair warning... it includes a pretty grisly murder.”

More clicks and clacks. “*Okay, I’ve got it onscreen.*” Longer pause as she apparently fast-forwarded through the last minute of David Simmonds’ life. “*Ugh, I did* not *need to see that when I was already queasy from go-juice overdose.*” Deep, steadying breath. “*Right, so check out the timestamp on the very last frame.*”

`2023-09-13T11:43:13+12`—September 13 at 11:43 a.m. Gray was already staring at it. “What am I looking for exactly?”

“*You see that plus-12 at the end? That’s the time zone. Plus-12 means UTC (England’s time zone, essentially) plus 12 hours, or if you prefer, twelve time zones east of England. As opposed to minus-8, or eight time zones* west *of England—which is the time zone I see on most of these other videos.*” Keyboard clacks. “*During Daylight Savings Time (which was active in September), minus-8 seems to correspond to Alaska and its coastal waters, including this Beaufort Sea you’re talking about.*”

Gray’s mind was already spinning through the implications of this. “So you’re telling me the September 13 timestamp is actually four hours different than what we thought it was? Like maybe the murder actually happened four hours later?” Yes, Gray decided, that was enough time for Dawn to wait an hour at the rendezvous and give up, having never seen David's yacht, *then* David show up, anchor his boat, and get murdered. It still left a lot of questions, and the timing was still too tight to instantly convince a jury of Dawn's innocence, but... it was a step in the right direction. It finally undermined the only un-fakeable evidence in the prosecution's case.

"*Four hours later?*" Bobbi repeated, then began laughing. "*Sure, man, you could say the murder happened four hours later than you thought... but on the previous day.*"

Gray froze.

"*These two time zones,*" Bobbi continued. "*They're on opposite sides of the International Date Line. They may only be a few hundred miles from each other, but they're 20 hours apart on the clock, usually on separate calendar days.*"

"I..." Gray was still speechless.

"*Yeah, man. Time zone math is super confusing, even to people in my line. Most folks don't even attempt it. Their eyes just glaze over.*"

"So... you're saying the timestamp superimposed on these videos was adjusted automatically based on David Simmonds' geographic location at the time each video was shot?" Gray demanded finally.

"*Yep, the time zone is always right there, clear as day in that plus-or-minus suffix that shows up after every timestamp,*" she confirmed. "*Obviously his computer was getting location data from his boat's*

GPS or whatever. And it looks like this guy moved around a lot, if he was crossing back and forth over the International Date Line."

Unbelievable. The linchpin he'd been looking for had been right in front of everyone's faces from the very beginning, if only they'd known what it meant. As for the cloud service techs, offering to testify in court, they surely *did* know what it meant, just not that they needed to explain it.

"So... when was David Simmonds actually murdered?" Gray asked slowly. "Can you calculate that for me?"

"*Way ahead of you, man,*" Bobbi said, amidst a flurry of keyboard clacks. "*This is converted to the Alaska time zone you seem to be expecting.*" And Gray's phone dinged from an incoming text message. He looked:

`2023-09-12T15:43:13-08`

"September 12 at 3:43 p.m.?" he asked, trying to keep the excitement out of his voice.

"*You got it, my man.*"

Gray's breath left him in a rush, and he sat back heavily. This indeed changed everything. The first text Dawn had received from David on September 12 had arrived at 3:58 p.m.—which Bobbi had now shown was fifteen minutes *after* David was already dead—incontrovertible proof that Dawn was being framed. But that also cleared up the inconsistency Gray kept running into, trying to profile the real killer.

Because the murder had not been premeditated after all... just the frame-job, which the killer had used the next 20 hours after the murder to plan and execute.

"Do you know what you've just done, Bobbi?" Gray asked his old friend quietly.

"*Blow this case wide open?*" she suggested eagerly.

"Blow this case wide open," he agreed, with an overwhelming surge of gratitude.

"*Excellent. Now go save the damsel in distress.*"

"Bobbi..." Gray began, then lapsed into laughter—deep, genuine laughter of a sort he hadn't experienced for some time. "Dawn would probably pop you in the nose for calling her a damsel. She'd be really nice about it, but..."

"*Oooh, I like her even better now. So go clear her name, then let* her *ask* you *out. Safer that way.*"

Gray could only laugh.

"*And then, Gray, call me back so we can catch up for real.*"

"Will do, Bobbi. I promise. And thank you."

"*Anytime, Double-G. Anytime.*"

Monday, January 15th

Utqiaġvik

Monday morning found Dawn, Samuel, and Esther standing before the superior court judge of Alaska's Second Judicial District, right here in Utqiaġvik's local courthouse. Standing next to the district attorney at the opposing counsel table were Detectives Jameson and Aiken. There was no jury present and never would be, if Gray got his wish.

Gray himself sat just behind the railing in the spectators' gallery, even though he himself was directly responsible for bringing this hearing about. After calling Samuel early Sunday to make him aware of his breakthrough, he had begun bombarding Jameson with calls and messages, then escalated to the district attorney, the judge's clerk, and ultimately the judge herself. This little campaign—on a Sunday, no less—hadn't won Gray any friends, which was exactly why he'd taken it upon himself instead of expecting it from Samuel, who needed to maintain good relations with everyone in this small town. But it had worked. By Sunday evening, an hour had been miraculously carved out of everyone's incredibly busy Monday schedules.

"And so you see," Samuel concluded his brief statement, "the murder actually occurred the day before—September 12 at 3:43 p.m. our time. Probably somewhere far to the west, across the International Date Line."

Gray was impressed. S. Taluġnaitchuk Leavitt, Esquire, cut an imposing figure in his sharp black suit, and he laid out the facts with concision and confidence.

At the lawyer's side, Dawn Atiqtalik Simmonds was also dressed professionally, in a neutral pantsuit—the first time Gray had ever seen her outside of flannel and denim, unless you counted the jumpsuit she was wearing at the jail on Christmas Day. The suit looked good on her, though she was quite tense, clearly still expecting the carpet to be pulled out from under her at any moment.

The judge turned toward the prosecution. "Is this true?" she asked. "David Simmonds was killed a whole day earlier than initially believed?" The DA opened his mouth to speak, but the judge waved her hand. "Not you. I'm asking them," she clarified, indicating Jameson and his partner.

Jameson looked a little embarrassed, but he nodded. "We had our own technical staff verify over the weekend. Mr. Simmonds *was* killed on September 12, according to the video footage we obtained."

"But you spent a month thinking it happened a whole day later. How was such a blunder possible?" the judge demanded.

There was an awkward silence as the prosecution tried to formulate an answer, and Samuel stepped into the gap. "It was an easy mistake to make," he admitted. "For the defense as well. We all took the timestamp at face value. And while I'd like to think one of the expert technical witnesses eventually called at trial would have cleared up the confusion, I'm just grateful that we can do so now. Before my client had to waste several more months of her life in jail, awaiting a court date."

This seemed to assuage the judge's very reasonable frustration at the injustice of the situation, and Jameson nodded gratefully to Samuel for his magnanimity. "So does this clear Ms. Simmonds of any suspicion regarding the murder of her brother?" the judge wanted to know.

"Not in and of itself..." the DA said leadingly.

Samuel produced a small stack of papers. "For that, we have sworn affidavits from multiple witnesses willing to testify to Ms. Simmonds' location on the *actual* day of the murder. She was in Nuiqsut all day, visiting family."

"Meaning she wasn't in the middle of the ocean far west of here, on her boat or anyone else's," the judge clarified.

"Not at what we now know was the actual date and time of the murder, correct." Samuel handed the affidavits to the clerk. "Ms. Simmonds was in Nuiqsut on the twelfth when Mr. Simmonds was murdered. That was also where she was when she apparently received a text message from her brother, luring her to a rendezvous out to sea on the following day. We now know Mr. Simmonds was already deceased by that time."

"So Ms. Simmonds was definitely framed?" the judge pressed, turning to the prosecution.

The detectives looked distinctly uncomfortable. "Maybe," Jameson said. "We still have DNA and ballistics evidence against Ms. Simmonds that points to her very clearly as the killer—"

"But," the DA broke in, "in light of the fact that someone claiming to be David Simmonds was sending the accused text messages from the victim's account fifteen minutes *after* we now know he was killed, it seems likely all other evidence against Ms. Simmonds was fabricated somehow also. Certainly someone else was involved."

"Who?" the judge demanded. "Who killed this man and then tried to frame his poor *sister* for it?"

Slowly, almost unwillingly, Jameson's gaze slid toward Gray, but the P.I. could only shrug. He still had no idea either. "We don't yet know," Detective Aiken spoke up. "But we will continue to investigate."

"What matters for today," the DA said, is that we see no reason to continue pursuing this case against Ms. Simmonds. Effective immediately, we are dropping all charges."

Dawn gasped with relief, despite knowing this was exactly where the hearing was supposed to conclude.

But the DA wasn't done. "*Including* the charges related to drug trafficking. Though that case against her still seems strong on the surface, the fact that someone has fabricated all this other evidence makes me question everything now."

"As well you should," the judge said sternly.

"I do, however, reserve the right to re-issue any drug-related charges against Ms. Simmonds in the future, pending the results of the NSBPD's ongoing investigation."

Gray felt a shiver run through him at this, but if Dawn felt the same, she gave no outward sign.

"Congratulations, Ms. Simmonds," the judge said formally, though her smile seemed genuine. "You're a free woman again. And may I be the first to apologize for the false accusations against you."

Overcome with emotion, Dawn could only nod in acknowledgment.

The judge rapped her gavel, and that was that.

Dawn leapt to her feet, except it wasn't to Samuel or Esther she turned first, but rather to Gray—and he saw her eyes were swimming with gratitude.

Grinning broadly, Gray extended a hand to her across the gallery railing, but Dawn slapped it away, enveloping him in a violent hug instead. "Thank you," she whispered hoarsely. "Thank you, thank you, thank you, thank you, *thank you.*"

Tuesday, January 16th

U-Turn

Following Dawn's release, Jameson arranged a fixed-wing Search & Rescue flight to return her to U-Turn on Tuesday morning. There were plenty of empty seats, so Gray was allowed to piggy-back on the free transportation, which was fortunate and timely—since his own regularly scheduled jetliner back to Anchorage was set to depart U-Turn just a few hours later.

But first, it was time to pay the piper. Gray had effectively gone AWOL from work the entire second week of this hitch, a fact that none of his crew would be quick to forgive, least of all Toolpusher Tim. In fact, after Gray's previous infraction, the termination of his employment seemed a foregone conclusion; and even if that weren't the case, Gray's broken arm would certainly prevent him from performing his usual duties for a long time to come. He needed this job, and P.I. work would never pay the bills in a place like this, so... Gray decided to bypass Tim and appear hat in hand before Mr. Thrasher, the big boss himself. After all, the company man had seemed supportive of

Gray's attempts to help Dawn, back when Gray and Abe Kanayurak met him in his office almost three weeks prior—even if, as it ultimately turned out, that interview had only led to more charges against Dawn.

After debarking the airstrip shuttle bus in U-Turn, Dawn reached for Gray in one more careful side hug—avoiding his injured right side—that lasted a little longer than was strictly necessary. "I'll see you again in two weeks then?" she asked, her eyes steady on his.

"Assuming I don't get fired, absolutely," Gray promised. "I'm more than ready for things to get back to normal. I've definitely missed your cooking, and I'm quite positive I'm not the only one."

She grinned, squeezed his left hand, then headed off toward her place with a spring in her step. And though the sky was dark as usual, only the faintest wisps of aurora borealis visible, U-Turn seemed brighter already for having her back.

With a sigh, Gray turned the other direction and began trudging toward his own fate at TrephOil HQ.

Soon, the roughneck 'fifth hand' was seated before Thrasher's hardwood power desk once again, staring at the knickknacks, awards, and photos while waiting for the company man to appear. He didn't have to wait long.

"Gaynes, is it?" Thrasher barked without preamble as he strode through the office door.

Gray jumped up so fast he almost kicked his chair over backwards. "Yes, sir."

Thrasher thrust out a hand to shake Gray's, and there was an awkward—and physically painful—moment as Gray tried to extend his own right arm, which was still immobilized in plaster cast and sling. Thrasher smoothly switched hands, seizing Gray's left in an iron grip, and clapping his other meaty paw on top for good measure. "I heard what you did for Dawn, what you risked for her, getting her cleared of suspicion—Abe told me all about it. Well done, and thank you, on behalf of myself and all of us at Treadgold-Phelps. I don't have to tell you what a wonderful person she is, and how much she and her restaurant do for company morale."

Gray felt like the other man was going to shake him right out of his skin, but he smiled with relief. It seemed that everything was going to work out okay for him after all. "Thank you, sir. I'm glad you see it that way."

"Of course, of course." Thrasher finally released him, rounding the desk to sit in his big leather chair and waving for Gray to retake his own seat. "And the police have no idea who *actually* murdered the brother? Abe couldn't—or wouldn't—tell me, but I imagine you're more current on the case anyway."

"No, sir, we have no idea," Gray admitted easily, surprised to realize that it didn't bother him overmuch. He hadn't set out to solve David's murder, after all, only to prove Dawn wasn't the one who'd committed it. That done, he was happy to throw away his remaining P.I. business cards. "Honestly, I question where the cops will even take the investigation from here. The entire timeline is blown out of the water. The only thing they really have to go on now is the killer's first name."

Thrasher snorted. "That's not much," he agreed. "Anyway, Suzanne told me about your situation, how you... uh... decided to prioritize Dawn's exoneration over your career here at Treadgold-Phelps." He chuckled.

"Yessir," Gray hurried to say. "It's not that I don't appreciate—"

"Save it, Gaynes, seriously. You're fine." He raised his voice, calling to his secretary out in the hall. "You hear that, Suzanne? Please make sure there are no black marks in Mr. Gaynes' employment record."

"Got it," a woman's voice called back, and Gray almost shook his head in relieved amusement. Everything was so casual here, unlike in his previous career at the NYPD.

That still didn't solve the rather glaring issue of Gray's broken arm and shoulder blade, however. The job of roughneck was physically demanding and absolutely required the use of both arms, yet Gray was looking at eight weeks recovery, minimum. "Is it possible I could get some sort of modified duty assignment for the time being?" he asked tentatively, indicating his cast and hoping he wasn't looking the gift horse in the mouth.

Thrasher eyed him musingly, then nodded. "A man like you, the kind that shows initiative and loyalty? I think we can do better than that. How about a promotion instead?" He stood abruptly, despite having only just sat down. Gray already knew this was a man who spent most of the workday on his feet. "C'mon, let's go talk to your supervisor—Tim something, right? We'll get everything all smoothed out. I know how the boys can be if they think you left them in the lurch, and I don't want that. They need to know you're a hero, flavor of the month, after what you did for Dawn."

Gray was smiling like an idiot. "Thank you, sir, genuinely. That means a lot to me."

"Of course," the company man assured him. "And once all that's settled, we'll see about getting you apprenticed to your crew's motorman. Ya know, one of the best motorhands I ever knew only had one arm, so I'm telling the truth when I say a man like you is more than capable of moving into that role." Thrasher was already standing in the door again. "Suzanne, you got all that? Promotion and special consideration?"

"Already typing it in Mr. Gaynes' file," came the secretary's voice. "But Don, don't forget you've got that 10 a.m. call with the home office."

"Shoot, yes," Thrasher said, checking his watch, then returning to his desk. "I'm sorry, Gaynes, I won't be able to walk you out after all. But I promise I'll get things sorted with your crew right afterwards.

They'll be buying you drinks at the airport bar in Anchorage as soon as you land, mark my words!"

But Gray wasn't marking the man's words at all anymore. He had only just stood from his own seat, and now his eyes fell slowly upon the engraved wooden nameplate situated so precisely on the company man's magnificent desk:

Ptolemy D. Thrasher

"Your middle name is Don?" Gray asked, straining to sound casual. "Or probably Donald, I guess? I, uh, have a cousin named Donald," he added lamely.

"It's Donnal, actually," Thrasher said with an easy laugh.

But that couldn't be right. Gray had searched TrephOil's master directory from right here in this very office, looking for any occurrence of D-O-N in an employee's name, and Thrasher had *not* come up.

"My parents were a bit kooky," Thrasher said, still chuckling. "Thought Ptolemy Donnal sounded like a conquering general and wanted to set me up for success." This time when the man said it, Gray heard the long-O and understood. Thrasher's middle name wasn't Donnal, but Domhnall—pronounced almost the same way, but spelled quite differently.

"That's a Gaelic name, isn't it?" Gray managed.

"Sure is, and you know those Scotch-Irish. Can't spell worth a damn. Imagine growing up with a name like that, more silent letters than a Charlie

Chaplin flick. Seriously, who does that to a kid?" He shrugged. "My friends just call me Don, and Suzanne does too. She's been with me forever."

Could it be? Could this man—Don Thrasher—be the same Don who murdered David Simmonds? Gray had always thought the oil field employees on his list of Dons seemed the *least* likely suspects, being itinerant, and with David only ever going ashore in Utqiaġvik. Dawn's brother simply didn't intersect with the oil industry, much less all the way down here in U-Turn.

But Dawn did. And someone had planted drugs and other evidence at Dawn's place. Someone, presumably, who could move around a small work camp like this without attracting notice as an outsider.

Someone like Ptolemy Domhnall Thrasher? An oil company executive who *wasn't* itinerant?

But why? What was his intersect with *David* Simmonds? What possible reason would a man like this have for harming a man like that?

Gray had been silent too long now, still standing before Thrasher's desk while the company man watched him curiously. Gray searched the other man's face. There was no hint of guilt, nothing but sincerity. And Gray realized he was being a fool. Even if Thrasher's name *was* Don, that didn't make him David's killer. It only seemed earthshattering in this moment because Gray hadn't realized until now.

Then again, Gray himself had just told Thrasher that the cops knew the killer's first name. And that name obviously sounded like *Dawn* or else they never would have arrested Dawn Simmonds. The company man was no idiot. He surely recognized why the sound of his given name had startled Gray. And to Gray's way of thinking, an innocent man would have immediately acknowledged the coincidence—with a laugh, perhaps—one way or another protesting his innocence.

But Thrasher hadn't done that. Because most guilty people just weren't very good at pretending the right kind of surprise when the unexpected occurred. And the company man hadn't acted guilty or surprised at all, even when he should have.

Instead, Don Thrasher just continued to smile—and Gray was suddenly eager to do exactly the same, rather than give any indication of his newfound suspicions. "Anyway, thank you again, sir."

"No, thank *you*, Gaynes. I look forward to seeing you out on the oil field." Then Thrasher gestured dismissively, reaching for his phone to dial into that 10 a.m. conference call.

And Gray staggered out of the office, ignoring the secretary's polite farewell. Moving in a daze, he stumbled the rest of the way through the HQ complex until he exited the front door into the darkness of midday outside.

Thrasher? Was *Thrasher* really the killer? No, surely not. Gray had no good reason to think so, outside of a gut feeling for how their conversation just now should have gone differently. Then again, after years of self-doubt, Gray's instincts had steered him right with Dawn. He shouldn't ignore his gut now.

But he couldn't simply report his new suspicions to the cops either. He'd seen first-hand the dangers of accusing a powerful person without proof. Doing that had been the beginning of Gray's downfall last time, during the Mad Batter investigation. Which left Gray exactly one option: to find the *evidence* to prove who actually killed David Simmonds, and to do it himself.

It seemed Gray's stint as a private investigator was not over yet after all.

First, though, Gray was long overdue for some rest and recovery, not to mention an extended visit from a lovely lady named Vera. Two weeks from today, he would fly back to U-Turn again, and that was soon enough to begin poking around for more answers.

But Gray had to be careful. If he *was* right about Thrasher, and Thrasher found out Gray was still snooping, the company man might just decide to commit another murder.

The stakes would never be higher than when Gray next set foot on the North Slope.

Gray Gaynes
will return in...

GRAY STAKES

Keep reading for a free preview!

FROM THE FILES OF

Gray Gaynes #8

GRAY STAKES

THE CASE OF THE IMPLAUSIBLE IMPALER

A NOVELLA BY

RL AKERS

Tuesday, January 30th
Anchorage, Alaska

Concourse C of the Ted Stevens Anchorage International Airport was an architectural marvel, evoking the rugged wonder of the Great State of Alaska with its craggy rock walls, natural lighting, and organic disdain for straight lines. Everywhere one turned, artistic murals hung interspersed with displays of taxidermied wildlife.

Grayson Gaynes—retired detective third grade, former roughneck 'fifth hand', now *what* he didn't know—tried not to look at the towering form of the nearby polar bear. Standing an incredible 12 feet tall, its fanged maw forever frozen in a furious rictus, the creature was even more terrible than the live one Gray had faced just three weeks prior. He couldn't help but shudder at the reminder of that traumatic experience.

Seated beside him in the Gate C2 waiting area, Vera Vecoli intuited Gray's discomfort and stood suddenly, moving to sit on his other side so he could turn away from the monster. He smiled gratefully. There were unknown depths of sensitivity to this woman that he never would have guessed when he met her that first time for dinner, now almost eight years prior in New York City. Then again, that was half a lifetime ago, and much had changed for both of them in the intervening years.

Now here she was, having followed him to Alaska, at least for these last two weeks. Her visit had been intended as a sort of test run to see if their long-postponed relationship was worth the long-distance investment.

As far as Gray was concerned, they had passed that test with flying colors.

Vera reached for Gray's hands, her grip tender since his entire right arm was still immobilized in a plaster cast and sling—another reminder of his kerfuffle with that bear. Now, though, without the specter of this bigger stuffed specimen looming over him, Gray's eyes were drawn more easily to Vera's. They were a deep brown, or so he'd been told, the shade complementary to her stylish brunette hair. Color blind as he was, what Gray perceived were twin depths of inky blackness that wanted to swallow him whole. He did not resist.

"I've enjoyed our time together," she told him. "Even more than I anticipated, and I had pretty high expectations."

"Your expectations are always set high," Gray told her lightly, drawing a throaty chuckle. "It's one of the many things I appreciate about you." He smiled. “I had a wonderful time too. I can’t believe it’s already over.”

Vera had arrived at this very airport two weeks ago today, the same day Gray himself got back from U-Turn, where he spent half of every winter month as an oil field worker. That was the day after Gray finally convinced authorities to drop murder and drug-related charges against his friend Dawn, and the very same day *he’d* begun to suspect that the real perpetrator was his boss’s boss’s boss—Don Thrasher, TrephOil’s top-ranking executive on the North Slope. Needless to say, as soon as they all got home from the airport, Vera and Old Gray (Gray’s father/housemate) had sat rapt for hours as Gray related the twists and turns of his previous six weeks on the North Slope.

Fortunately, that hadn’t been the most exciting thing to come of Vera’s first visit to Alaska. Gray and Vera’s days together had been occupied with word games and puzzles at the Gaynes’ house in Eagle River, or hiking Anchorage’s many picturesque trails; and their evenings by dressy fine dining experiences, live opera, and even a touring production of the Broadway musical *Hamilton*. In short, the time Gray had spent with Vera was quite a bit more sophisticated than what he generally enjoyed above the Arctic Circle. Not better, per se, but a little closer to the cultured existence he’d aspired to during his old life.

He’d genuinely enjoyed every minute of it. It was still early days, but... well, Gray was finding it easier than ever to picture a future with this stunning woman. One that didn't feel like he was dishonoring his late wife, Rose.

And now the two of them were forced to say goodbye. Within the next few minutes, Vera's flight back to JFK would begin boarding here at C2; then, Gray would have just enough time to reach C7 for his own biweekly commute between Anchorage and U-Turn.

Gray and Vera had talked of so much during the last two weeks, never struggling to find a new topic, but suddenly Gray couldn't think of a thing to say. The silence hung awkward between them, until he cleared his throat. "There's just one thing I'm still wondering," he said hesitantly.

"What's that?" Vera asked with a sly smile.

He took a deep breath, then leaned forward. Her eyes widened with delight, and she met him halfway. They kissed, and for a long moment, everything else in Gray's world faded.

Then he was ripped out of the moment by a nearby explosion of whoops and cheers. "Get 'er, Gaynes!" someone cried as the kiss came to a premature end.

"Who's that?" Vera asked, smiling hesitantly as she eyed the passing group of men.

"I'm not 100% sure," Gray said, even as he exchanged friendly waves with a few. "Some of the guys from work, I assume."

"You're not going to introduce me?"

"No." Gray watched as the other oil field workers, still talking and joking amongst themselves, continued up the concourse and out of sight. "Introductions would be sorta tough, considering..."

"Considering you're prospagnostic?" she tried.

He barked a laugh. "Prosopagnosic, yes."

"I still think that's crazy," she wondered aloud, for probably the dozenth time since rekindling their relationship. "I mean, you really don't recognize *anyone*'s face?" She cocked her head playfully. "How do you even know that I'm me?"

"Aside from the fact that you've been with me this entire time?" he asked drily.

"Aside from that, yes."

"Well, let's see." He happily seized the excuse to admire Vera's features: her creamy, unblemished skin; that graceful nose centered between delicate high cheekbones; her big, dark eyes and elegant neck. It wasn't that her face was somehow fuzzy or indistinct to his eyes. He could appreciate her classical beauty with perfect clarity, and indeed, her proximity stirred something primal within him. Yet it was like looking on the face of a stranger, even though he'd been at her side every waking hour of the last half month. "I'm actually not entirely sure that it *is* you," he admitted with a joking frown.

She arched an eyebrow, then gave him a whole sequence of silly, over-the-top winks—left eye three times, right eye once, then back to left—before tugging at her right ear lobe. This was, of course, the bit of ridiculous spycraft they had developed for exactly this purpose. It had actually proven helpful after she used the restroom at the opera, too.

"Oh, Vera!" he said in mock relief. "It *is* you."

She grinned, though the smile faded after a moment. "So your coworkers don't know? About your thing with faces, I mean."

He shrugged. "No reason they need to."

"But I didn't think you were keeping it a secret anymore. It's practically public knowledge anyway," she pressed. "Gray, you took down a serial killer. There's a wiki article about you and everything."

"Which they *definitely* don't need to know," he said, laughing. "Don't worry, I've made a few real friends in my time here, and I've been open with them about my past, about my... frailties. But the guys on my crew, we keep things pretty surface level."

Vera nodded slowly, then hesitated, speaking with forced casualness. "And these true friends of yours... they include Dawn? The woman you just got out of jail?"

"Sure," Gray said. "I would count her in that group." He felt he should reassure Vera that 'friend' was all Dawn was, that maybe this reassurance was exactly what Vera wanted to hear. But trying to put that into words made him uncomfortable, so he just changed the subject. "What were we talking about before?" he asked leadingly.

Vera's smile turned predatory, and this time she was the one to initiate the kiss. Fortunately, there were no further interruptions.

At last, she sat back with a contented sigh. "I'm glad to know that works for both of us."

Gray's heart was racing. "Yeah," he agreed hoarsely, trying not to let on how short of breath he was. Today was, after all, the first they'd kissed. Some might think that old fashioned, waiting so long, especially after months of phone calls and two weeks of continual in-person interaction. To Gray's way of thinking, it felt recklessly fast, considering it *was* only two weeks of actually seeing one another. But then, he wasn't sure when he would see her next.

The PA crackled, the gate agent announcing the boarding of Vera's flight—for which she got to board in zone one, thanks to all the business travel she did.

"You're first class in every way," Gray quipped lamely as they stood. "I'm... gonna miss you," he added in a more earnest tone.

She smiled brilliantly. "Do me a favor and call me sometime."

He blinked. "Of course I will."

"*More* than once a month?"

Gray grinned. "I promise."

Vera squeezed him one last time, then pulled away quickly and strode up to the gate agent.

Boarding pass scanned, she gave Gray another sequence of silly winks, then she was out of sight up the jet bridge.

Gray turned toward his own gate with mixed feelings. He was so excited about the future of this relationship, yet discouraged knowing he wouldn't see Vera again for quite some time. Plus, now he had to go back to work, his exact role uncertain thanks to his injury. At Gray's last meeting with the big boss, Mr. Thrasher had generously offered to get Gray on-the-job training in a new position—just moments before something *else* he said triggered Gray's old homicide detective instincts. It was now widely known that a webcam recording existed of the David Simmonds murder from last September, in which the victim referred to his killer as 'Don' (one of the reasons David's sister Dawn was initially arrested); but it wasn't so widely known that Ptolemy Domhnall Thrasher also went by 'Don,' at least among his friends. And while that was hardly suspicious in and of itself, Thrasher's complete failure to acknowledge the coincidence *did* raise Gray's suspicions dramatically. Still, even if Thrasher was a killer (and Gray had said nothing to suggest he thought so), that didn't mean *Gray* had to do anything about it. He had already accomplished everything he set out to do last month, clearing Dawn of guilt. Was proving Thrasher's guilt instead really what he wanted to do next? *That* certainly wasn't Gray's job anymore. Whatever he was now, he was no longer a cop.

So... yeah. All of *those* questions and worries were contributing to Gray's emotional conflict too.

One thing was sure, at least. Gray was about to get a full ribbing from his coworkers, considering what they'd just seen of him and Vera. He would have to resume his usual song and dance of pretending he recognized people, while avoiding any deeper conversation that might reveal he didn't. There really wasn't any big reason he couldn't tell the guys about his conditions, except that... well, Gray rather feared the pranks that might ensue. On the other hand, that was nothing compared to his worries about Thrasher.

But when Gray arrived at Gate C7, the welcome he got wasn't anything like what he expected. "Gaynes, get over here!" called one man. And when Gray complied, a dozen or more of the others enveloped him with intent expressions.

"Uh, what's going on?" Gray asked, glancing around uncomfortably. There was something electric in the air, and it went beyond the small cluster of roughnecks around him. More than 150 men congregated at this gate, awaiting the imminent boarding announcement, and it seemed every one of them was talking with nervous excitement.

"You seriously don't know?" demanded the guy who had called him over.

Gray bent to set down his carry-on, using the motion as cover for a furtive glance at the luggage tag on that fellow's bag. "No, Miller, I seriously don't know," Gray answered levelly as he stood.

The man everyone called Motormouth Miller shook his cell phone at Gray. "You don't check your messages?"

"Not in the last hour or so," Gray admitted.

"He was too busy sucking face!" someone else pointed out, leading to a healthy round of guffaws.

Gray couldn't help but smile. "Guilty as charged." There. Ribbing accomplished. "What is it? What's going on?" he repeated.

"Email came from Corporate a few minutes ago. They want us to be prepared when we land. Apparently—"

"There's been another murder," one of the other guys blurted.

Gray recoiled. "On the North Slope?"

"In U-Turn!" someone else said in an excited, semi-reverent whisper.

"Who?" Gray demanded.

"I dunno, some security guy—"

"Harmon Freyes," Miller interjected with strained patience. "According to the memo from Corporate. Didn't *anyone* actually read it?"

Gray frowned. Why did that name sound familiar? Then it clicked. Harmon Freyes was the friendly blond giant sent by company security to help arrest that drug mule Gray identified last month, when he was working to clear Dawn's name. Gray's face fell. "What happened? Some sort of security incident?" It wasn't unheard of for malcontents to attack oil drilling sites, as a form of eco-terrorism or just to steal crude oil. That kind of thing was much less common in the remote, frigid North Slope, but it remained a risk—which was why Treadgold-Phelps and companies like it employed so many well-equipped security personnel. "Did Harmon get shot or something?"

"Corporate didn't say," Miller admitted.

"But what we heard, it's *strange*," said a dark-skinned man—probably their crew's EMT, Cedrick—before stopping for a completely inappropriate dramatic pause.

"Strange *how*," Gray pressed impatiently.

Everyone turned to face another guy—Frampton the machinist, Gray decided, based on the mole above his left eye. "Well, I got a buddy's got a buddy knows a guy coming off hitch," Frampton said slowly. "And *he* says old Freyes came hurtling into town on a snowmobile this morning, just as everyone was loading onto the buses for the ride to the airstrip. *He* says Freyes was covered with blood, half dead even before he crashed into one of the modulars. They called for the doc, but it was already too late."

"But he hadn't been shot," maybe-Cedrick said, demanding everyone's attention again. "According to Frampton's buddy—"

"I don't know him personally—" Frampton tried to correct.

Cedrick waved away the correction impatiently. "Freyes wasn't shot. He was *stabbed*." He paused once more for effect, clenching a fist and lifting it high. "Harmon Freyes had a wooden stake driven straight through his chest."

Gray looked around, realizing that all the guys on his crew were again staring at *him*, crowding Gray specifically. "So..."

"So we want to know," Miller concluded intensely. "What are you gonna do about it?"

Gray's eyes widened. "Me?"

"Yeah, you. You solved the last murder." Gray had done nothing of the kind, of course, only proving that Dawn couldn't have been the murderer. But that wasn't a distinction Miller or the others really cared about. "So now," Miller concluded, glancing around the circle of rough and tumble workers before returning his gaze to Gray. "Are you gonna solve this murder too?"

Acknowledgments

Attempting to write a story like this one, set in a place—and at a confluence of cultures—so outside my personal experience, would have been unthinkable without the immense assistance of a North Slope local. Words cannot express my appreciation for Trish Sukren Brower for her patience and enthusiasm throughout the course of our months-long discourse about Iñupiat customs and culture (and naming conventions!) as well as all things North Slope Borough. Only through Trish's copious first-person insights was I able to bring her homeland to life to even a fraction of the degree it deserves. It probably goes without saying, but any errors in fact or nuance pertaining to this book's setting and people are solely mine. And while U-Turn and TrephOil specifically are fictional inventions, much of the credit (and none of the blame) is still due to Trish for helping me craft a plausible work camp and company modeled after real world examples.

Many thanks also go to Brenna Cox, for initial discussions about Alaska and Native Alaskan culture, for making my introduction to Trish, and for proofing a draft of the story and offering feedback of her own.

Thank you to Tom and Becky Poling for their unique perspective as long-term transplants to America's Last Frontier. Their knowledge of the most desirable neighborhoods and establishments in

Anchorage was helpful, as were the various edits they suggested to my first draft, helping me paint a more accurate picture of life in Alaska. Their expertise regarding the most commonly carried firearms and ammunition (and all that entailed for my story) also proved vital. Meet you on the battlefield, guys!

In a similar vein, thank you to Bill Coleman for his quick assistance in a pinch with regard to one passage.

Drew Senter offered a *lot* of great suggestions that improved this book across the board, though I was originally just looking for his perspective on the life and practice of a lawyer in a small town. He helped me address various items that were unrealistic, and otherwise develop Samuel into a more well-rounded and consistent character. Thanks, Drew, for caring about this book as much as you do!

I'm always grateful to Matt Santen for his responsiveness and feedback on early drafts of each new Gray story. This time around, his sheer enthusiasm for both Gray and Alaska—reminding me of past books' details regarding the former, and informing me of random trivia about the latter—ensured I didn't make any major factual mistakes. Oh, and thanks for finally clearing me up on the difference between 'off-Broadway' and 'touring.'

My parents, Ruth and Les Akers, provided their usual service of catching typos and mixed-up homophones, as well as identifying instances in which reasonable readers might miss my implications or simply misunderstand the intent of my writing. Thank you for everything you've done in the last 4+ decades to minimize distractions and heighten engagement within my prose.

Regarding the preview chapter for *Gray Stakes*, it was my daughter Sadie's obsession with *Hamilton* that resulted in its inclusion (that and the fact that it *did* play in Anchorage that season!). Thanks to you, Sadie, it seems one or another of that show's songs is often stuck in my head, and this is what comes of it. Now I need to hurry up and write the rest of Gray's eighth adventure, whether or not I'm running out of time.

And, of course, my wife Sarah remains my partner in all I do. Thank you for being so eager (and rather demanding, this time around!) to read this reboot of Gray's adventures, for catching all the earliest typos that made it through my own proofing, and for raising reasonable concerns about possible plot holes and other immersion-breaking issues—then on the back end of the process, being my last line of defense for proofing final edits to ensure I don't create all-new problems! I am as thrilled as ever to be on this adventure with you.

Also by R.L. Akers:

GRAY IN THE CITY

The first Gray Gaynes
anthology collection includes:

1. ***Gray Tones:*** *The Case of the Elevator Slaying*
2. ***Gray Area:*** *The Case of the Hellhound Homicide*
3. ***Old Gray:*** *The Case of the Cold-Blooded Cremation*
4. ***Gray Matter:*** *The Case of the Autonomous Assassination*
5. ***Gray Rose:*** *The Return of the Mad Batter*
6. ***Fade to Gray:*** *The Fate of the Vengeful Victim*

and the exclusive short stories:

- "Black & White"
- "Rose-Colored Glasses"

Meet GRAY GAYNES:

A brilliant investigator, but also a man deeply wounded by his own personal tragedy... An NYPD homicide detective willing to go to great lengths to hide the truth of the irrevocable changes he is undergoing, and to identify the man that murdered his wife before his very eyes. If only Gray had any recollection of that terrible day...

FROM THE FILES OF

ANTHOLOGY

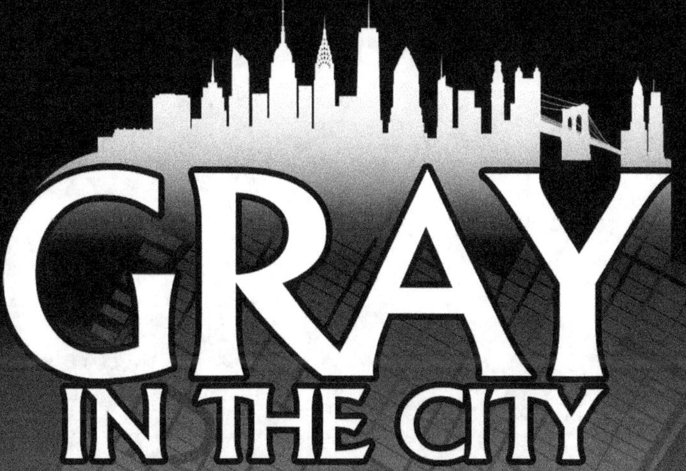

THE COMPLETE SERIES OF
NYPD DETECTIVE
MURDER MYSTERIES

SIX NOVELLAS
AND TWO EXCLUSIVE SHORT STORIES
BY
RLAKERS

AKERS THE KING OF CAYMERLOT

AKERS THE HEROES OF GENTHULE

AKERS THE CIRCUS OF DAGMØR

AKERS ESCAPE FROM OVERTWIXT

AKERS OVERTWIXT

RL AKERS

OVERTWIXT™

WELCOME TO THE WORLD OF BRIDGES

ILLUSTRATED BY Jesse Lewis

OVERTWIXT™

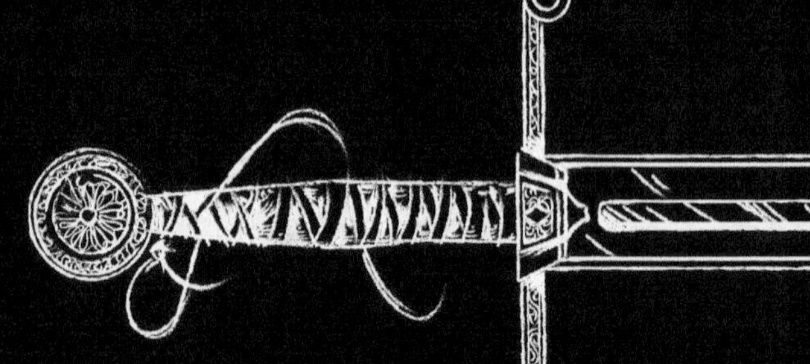

Also by R.L. Akers:

OVERTWIXT

In the words of the Guide, "Overtwixt is the world of bridges, where all parallel universes intersect." It is a place of wonder, where strange bridges link floating islands that are populated by bizarre peoples. In Overtwixt, adventure and excitement abound... along with sword fights, magic, witty banter, and positive moral messages for young adult (YA) readers.

Overtwixt: The World of Bridges and ***Escape from Overtwixt*** relate the modern-day story of four siblings' arrival in Overtwixt, after they step through the wrong gate at the airport. They must overcome challenges and prejudice to unite the realm and overthrow an evil dictator. Both books are around 65,000 words.

Circus of Dagmør, ***Heroes of Centhule***, and ***King of Caymerlot*** comprise the Golden Age trilogy of prequel novels, set in Overtwixt about 3,000 years before the modern age. These books tell the tale of a troupe of circus performers and their friends who get caught up in larger events when an army of giant barbarians attacks — which provides fun historical backstory to some of the situations in the modern-day books. All three prequel books are between 75,000 and 105,000 words.

Visit Overtwixt.com or online retailers for details about these novels and other tie-in books.

Also by R.L. Akers:

ATLANTIS: Twilight of Mankind

In a time before recorded history, most of humankind lives in close proximity to a single magnificent City located on the Isle of Atalas. Ruled directly by a Pantholon of twenty-three gods, society remains in a pre-industrialized state, but great strides have been made in the realms of engineering and genetics.

In pursuit of absolute power, one of the four ruling members of the Pantholon sends his demigod son D'Akaio on a series of missions designed to undermine his rivals; as D'Akaio's fame grows among the common people, so too do the stories told about him (eventually becoming the very legends that informed Norse, Egyptian, and Greco-Roman mythology).

Meanwhile, D'Akaio's half-sister Adana launches her own private war against the Pantholon, working with an underground resistance movement to quietly rescue the women and children who are scheduled for sacrifice before the gods.

Events build toward a confrontation between brother and sister, even as the City and its depraved society speed toward prophesied doom.

Read this all-new contribution to the lore surrounding everyone's favorite lost city, on sale now!

Visit Isle-of-Atlantis.com or online retailers for details.

RLAKERS

ATLÅNTIS

TWILIGHT OF MANKIND

Best Seller

A NOVEL

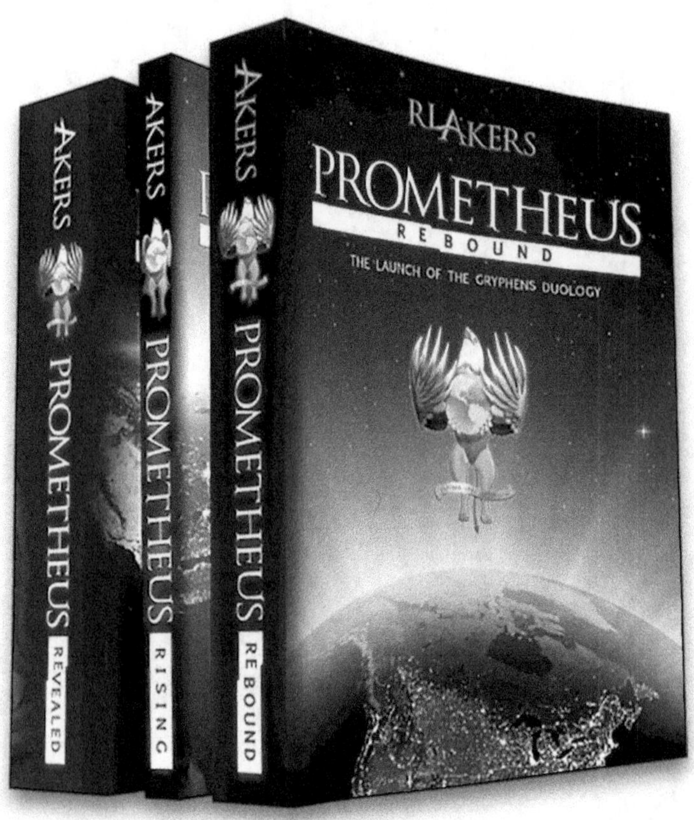

The Gryphens Saga consists of the novels ***Prometheus Rebound*** *and* ***Prometheus Revealed****, along with the short story collection* ***Prometheus Rising****. All three volumes are on sale now.*

Visit Gryphens.com or online retailers for details.
Visit OrbitalDefense.com to jump straight into the story!

Also by R.L. Akers:

The GRYPHENS SAGA

You've seen the big-budget summer action flicks. You've read the books, maybe played the video games. You've heard all the conspiracy theories. But this is the real world, the present day. If the unthinkable happened, if we faced an actual, verifiable threat from outside our planet...

What would we do?
The Gryphens Saga tells that tale.

Blending military thriller and science fiction—with an emphasis on the science—R.L. Akers produces a well-crafted story peopled by characters you'll grow to love and hate. When the threat from outer space becomes known, the U.S. government is caught unprepared. With time running out, the military must adapt to an entirely new variety of warfare. Pilots and soldiers must be recruited, trained, and deployed to defensive installations in orbit above North America, and technology must take a giant leap forward… with considerable assistance from a surprising source.

But there are those who would halt these preparations: mercenaries and even traitors within the ranks. What motivates them to betray their world is unknown, but they will stop at nothing to prevent the newest branch of United States military from fulfilling its mandate.

From the shadows of rural England to the bowels of Area 51's Groom Lake installation, from the most remote corner of our planet to geosynchronous orbit thousands of miles above, the Gryphens Saga comprises a single well-researched and believable story about humanity's real-world response to the threat of alien invasion. You won't want to put these books down!

Lisa Dawn Thompson

R.L. Akers loves stories. He loves hearing them, telling them, embellishing them, and forging them from raw materials. He remains convinced that every person who ever lived has an interesting story, including that one guy who tried and failed to prove otherwise.

Holder of an undergraduate degree in computer science and a master's degree in business administration, Akers has worked in software development as well as non-profit fundraising and publicity. He loves children and has served them in various capacities over the years, both at his church and within the foster care system. His interests include graphic design, orchestral movie soundtracks, home improvement, and other creative pursuits.

Akers lives in West Virginia with his wife Sarah and the four children he loves most in this world... except when some of them are off at college. Visit him online at RLAkers.com.

www.ingramcontent.com/pod-product-compliance
Lightning Source LLC
LaVergne TN
LVHW020706110826
845149LV00012B/2131

* 9 7 9 8 9 9 3 3 7 3 2 2 5 *